DEATH ON THE ROCKS

An Australian Historical Fiction Novella

The Australian Sandstone Series

MICHAEL BEASHEL

Title: Death on The Rocks
Series: The Australian Sandstone Series
Author: Michael Beashel

Publishing and Marketing Consultant: Lama Jabr
Website: https://xanapublishingandmarketing.com
Sydney, Australia

Cover by Giovanni Banfi
Image: 2 Cambridge Street looking South 1902 Artist Fred Leist'.

Contents

The Rocks Sydney -early 1800s

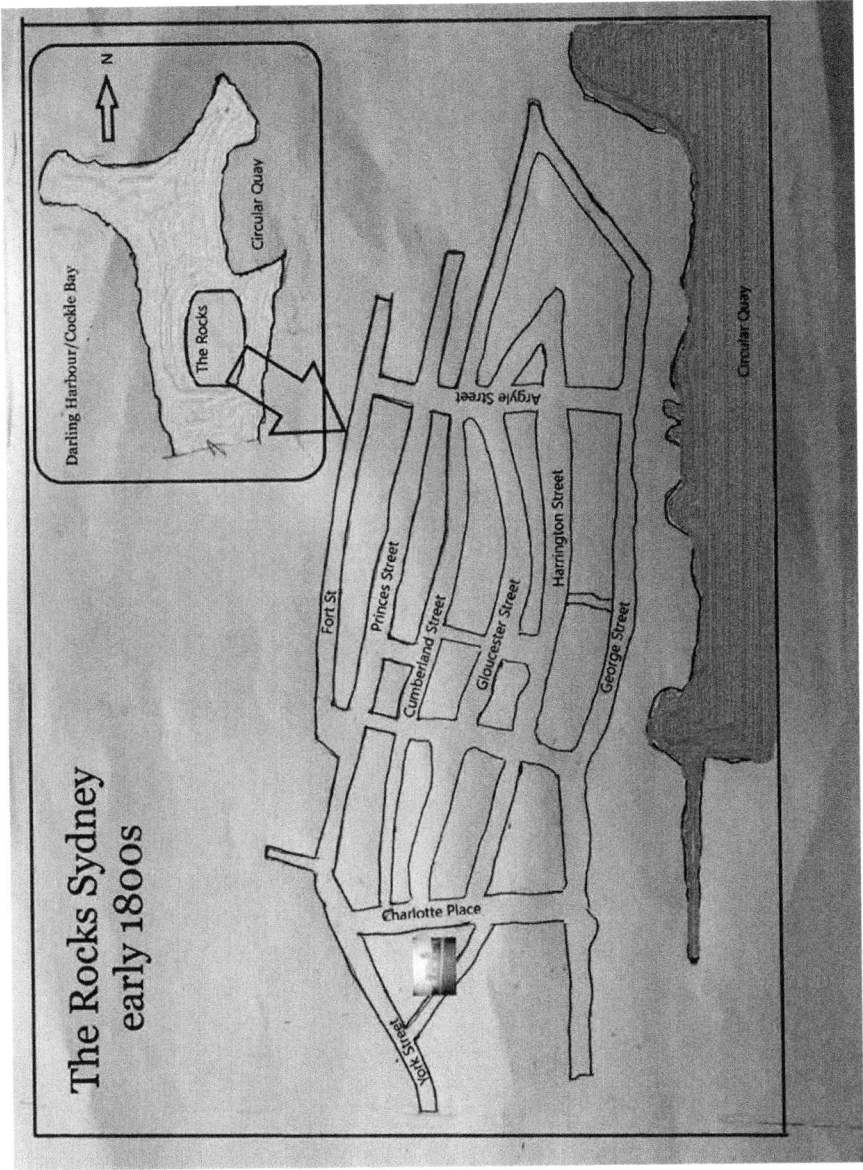

The Rocks Sydney early 1800s

N

Darling Harbour/Cockle Bay

The Rocks

Circular Quay

Circular Quay

Argyle Street

Fort St

Princes Street

Cumberland Street

Gloucester Street

Harrington Street

George Street

Charlotte Place

York Street

Chapter One

1823

The night air was thick with humidity, cloaking the western promontory of Port Jackson known as The Rocks. There was no breeze and the windows of the New Liffey hotel, opening to Cumberland Street, let in insects and street smells that mingled with those of the bar room. Judith Sampson, the landlady, smiled to herself. This weather was to be expected in Sydney just three days before Christmas. Leaving the bar, she circulated among the nine tables of seated and noisy patrons, collecting empty glasses, keeping an eye on suspected pickpockets and an ear open for noisy drinkers who could erupt to a fight more quickly than a kookaburra swooping on prey.

'Hot night, Mrs Sampson,' said a red-faced patron, raising his empty glass to her.

'It won't get any cooler before closing, sir. So, you'd better fill that mug.'

'That I'll do. That I'll do.'

Juggling ten glasses, Judith returned to the bar, where her barman was serving the New Liffey's popular beer, made on the premises. Grabbing a cloth, she wiped the bar top down to the end, where one of her lodgers, seated on a stool, was leaning against the wall.

'How are you liking the town?' Judith asked.

'In the two days I've been here, ma'am, it's an interesting place.' The man put his half-filled glass down and ran his fingers through his blond hair, which was clubbed, tied back into a leather band. He smiled at her. 'But I've not had much chance to do anything but work.'

Judith placed her empty glasses onto a draining board alongside the sink under the bar. She started washing them. 'How long will you be in Sydney?'

'It depends on whether we get the right timber. We would prefer teak or oak. But there's none here, so we have to accept your native hardwoods.'

'Can you work with those, to fix the damage to your ship?'

'We can, ma'am, but timber like that is more difficult to shape.' The man finished his drink and held out his glass. 'One more please, ma'am.'

'Surely.'

Judith liked the lilting voice of this customer, who looked to be in his early twenties. By a woman of thirty like herself, or any woman for that matter, David Milligan would be thought handsome. He stood out: a six-foot frame, all muscle, a tanned face with even features, a cheeky smile. She glanced at him as she pulled the beer. And he had more than good looks. His speech was not of the rough sort that she expected from a whaler; it had an educated tone to it. She placed the beer back on the bar. 'What part of America are you from?'

'Boston, Massachusetts, ma'am.' Milligan gave her a coin. 'The sea called me, and I answered it. I'm a mechanic.' That was a term for any specialist who worked on whaling ships. 'A carpenter, for my troubles. Myself and the boys are fixing up a larboard hole, courtesy of an uncharted reef on your south coast.' He took a generous gulp of his beer. 'And how long have you been in Sydney yourself, ma'am?'

She was about to answer when Michael came up behind her. She gave a little start: Michael had been in Parramatta buying supplies and she hadn't seen him all week.

Not unhappy about surprising her, he gave her a grin. 'Here, love, I'll finish those.' He grabbed a towel and started wiping the glasses.

'Thank you, dear,' Judith said. 'Good to see you back at work. You're in time to meet our new lodger.'

The carpenter-mechanic stood up and put out his right hand. 'David Milligan is my name, sir. I'm from the Nantucket whaler, *Cyprus*, that's docked in Cockle Bay for repair.'

Michael smiled. 'Pleased to meet you, Mr Milligan. I'm Michael Sampson, husband of the delightful and attractive publican standing beside me.'

'Get on with you,' Judith said. She coloured, though pleased with the compliment. 'You're embarrassing me.'

'If Mr Sampson will permit me, ma'am, I agree with the sentiment.' Milligan sipped his beer and looked at them both. 'So, how long have you been in the colony?'

Judith glanced at her husband. 'I've been here for ten years and Michael since 1810.'

'Forgive my directness, ma'am, but did you both come as free settlers?'

'I did,' Michael Sampson said. 'My wife was transported here for the heinous crime of lifting a yard of ribbon.'

Milligan shook his head. 'Extraordinary.' He looked around. 'You've both done well in that time. With this pub and all.'

'That we have,' Michael said, 'and we have the best beer in The Rocks, made here and served by the best-looking—'

'There's more empties to get, Michael,' Judith said. 'Best be at it.'

'Yes, Boss.' Michael smirked and left them.

Milligan said with a sigh, 'I have an early mark in the morning, ma'am, so please excuse me.'

'Goodnight, Mr Milligan,' Judith said and watched him go up the stairs to the hotel's rooms. These were always occupied, because The Rocks, with its shacks, huts, houses, workshops and businesses all jammed together along its steep, narrow streets, saw an everlasting flow of people passing through, from the harbour to the settlements beyond, or back to the harbour again and away to sea.

Michael brought some empties to the bar. 'He doesn't talk like a sailor, does he?'

'That he does not,' Judith said. 'More like a teacher at some fancy American school. Maybe he went to Boston to study, did something against the law and then hopped it.'

Michael Sampson laughed. 'You and your imagination, Judith, really. Now, I'll be in the cellar.'

'Don't be long. You're needed back here. I've got to duck up and see that the children are asleep.'

Michael waved an acknowledgement and headed for the cellar; a twenty-foot square cave dug out of the sandstone of the promontory.

Judith served a new customer and thought about the whaler. He'd turn women's heads while he was in town. Whom had he left behind in America—a wife, perhaps? Would that stop him looking for a good time here, while he was on the other side of the world? He was an attractive man.

* * *

Thomas Wilson dismounted from his horse and led it towards the stable behind his George Street house. The rest of the space between the back of the house and the rear fence, which adjoined a lane, was a generous garden, planted with lemon trees, tomato vines, carrots, strawberries and lettuces, all set out among camellias, gardenias, roses and magnolias. It was his wife's Anne's pride and joy and envied by his neighbours.

It had been a long ride from Toongabbie and the barley fields. The colony was expanding and more land, west of Parramatta, had come into use to supply the needs of a growing population. He'd spent the last three weeks in the Toongabbie area, inspecting the farms, interrogating the farmers who were contracted to him, and examining the stored barley to assure himself that both its quantity and quality were up to the standard he required for purchase. No smooth-talking farmer would convince him that the crop they had gathered was good for his purposes. No, he himself had to smell the product and feel it, and that he had done. At forty-two years he had learnt how to deal with men, and whenever necessary he would confront those bigger and taller than his own five feet six inches.

Handing his horse to his stable boy, he said, 'Give him a feed and water and clean him up.' The boy nodded and waited as Wilson undid his saddlebags.

Wilson left the stable with his bags and paused before he entered the back door of his house, glancing aside to appreciate a glimpse of the harbour that he could see from the doorstep, between his house and the next.

The harbour below the town glittered in the early evening, reminding him of what he had achieved since his voyage out in 1815, when he followed his desire to emigrate from London and take advantage of the prospects in New South Wales. He smiled; no Putney land could give him what he had now. Sure, he didn't own the land that the precious barley and hops were grown on, but he had the next best thing in his hands: product. Product that was in demand, and few men could beat him in its exploitation.

After Christmas, he'd do a final inspection of the crops out west and then arrange for wagons to bring the Toongabbie barley and hops to town. They would bring him bright coin when he sold them on to the grain buyers in Sydney. In turn, the retailers made their own profit by selling the grain on to the hotels and breweries—but they were dependent on him to get the product to their doors, and they needed frequent deliveries, because Sydney drinkers were a thirsty bunch.

There seemed no limit to the amount of barley and hops that Wilson could bring into Sydney, provided he could find new farmers to grow it. Why, if he had one thousand acres to source, it would still not be enough to satisfy the need of the twelve-thousand-strong population, twelve hundred of whom lived right here around him in The Rocks. Traders in Sydney found it most convenient to buy from him, and for that convenience they were willing to pay his prices.

There was just one trader who tried to drive a hard bargain and give him grief on every exchange, and that was Mr Peter Ryan. He sought to wear Wilson down by complaining about the quality of his grain, and threatening to find another trader who could give him better for a lower price. Wilson, having got an early hold on the ways to bring good quantities of grain into town, and knowing the other traders would never be real competition for him, stuck to his guns on price and got his due payment, but his patience with Ryan was wearing thin.

Wilson went through the back door of his house, placed his bags down on the floor for a servant to pick up, and went into the parlour.

'I thought it might be you,' a voice greeted him.

'Hello, Anne,' Wilson said, and turned to see her sitting near the window where the light was good for her hand-sewing.

'How was the trip?' she said serenely, without getting out of her chair.

He gave a wry smile. There were plenty of dangers facing a man who went all the way west to Toongabbie and back, attacks by bushrangers being one of them, but his wife seemed to think he could cope with anything, and never looked worried on his departure or especially relieved on his arrival.

He shrugged and sat down in a generously padded chair. 'I'm bushed. I stopped the night in Ashfield but it's still a long ride from there.'

His wife gave him a sympathetic smile. 'Have you eaten?'

'No.'

'Then I'll ask Cook to get you something.' She got up to go to the kitchen.

'Thank you.' Wilson sat back and reached for the *Gazette* on the table beside him. He turned to the grain prices and started to read.

Footsteps made him look up. 'Good evening, Father, welcome back.'

Wilson smiled at his daughter. She was eighteen, petite but full-figured, with lively brown eyes in a clear-skinned complexion. Her brunette hair was up in a bun today and she looked somehow more grown up. He had missed her. 'Thank you, my dear. How have you been?'

Jane Wilson sat on the edge of the opposite armchair. She brought out a handkerchief and dabbed her forehead. 'I've been all right. This sticky heat! Worse than last year. We'll swelter over Christmas dinner. How was your trip?'

They chatted for a while, and when the meal was ready on the table in the dining room, Anne Wilson came into the parlour. 'Come and have your meal, and we'll join you. Have you washed up yet?'

Wilson stood up. 'I'll do that now.'

Ten minutes later, refreshed, Wilson attacked the lamb stew. He said to his wife, 'Out west was even hotter than this. You could have fried an egg on one of my shovels. Still, I liked what I found—the barley crop this year is good. We won't be short of the ready. You'll be able to buy those new fabrics you wanted.' He smiled at his daughter. 'Jane, you'll be able to afford new silk dresses.'

'Very good,' Anne said, and Jane smiled.

He went on with his meal. 'Where is Henry?'

'Your son is dining with the Campbells tonight,' Anne said.

Wilson's ears pricked up. '*The* Campbells?' Robert Campbell was a rich merchant, whose storehouses stood not sixty yards from the Wilson house. Campbell was a close associate of Governor Brisbane, and an excellent man for Wilson's twenty-one-year-old son to know.

Anne smiled and nodded. 'Indeed. He seems to have joined their set.'

'All well and good.' Wilson went on to talk about his three weeks' stay out west and they also talked about Christmas, two days away.

* * *

Judith Sampson closed the New Liffey hotel for four hours in the middle of Christmas Day, a decision she and Michael had taken together. The Lord's birthday deserved to be celebrated in their own private way. Thus, at eleven am on Thursday, 25 December 1823, the doors were shut and the only people allowed inside with the Sampson family were five friends and the four men who lodged at the hotel.

By twelve-thirty, these allotted people were seated and tucking into roast turkey, roast chicken and lamb, with gravy and baked potatoes. All washed down with New Liffey ale. David Milligan was seated at Judith's left hand, while at the opposite end of the table sat her husband Michael, who was in deep conversation with one of their friends. On Judith's right were their two children, five-year-old Liam, and Maeve, who was nearly three. Liam was playing with a small wooden boat.

'That's a special gift you've given Liam, Mr Milligan,' Judith said, looking at the model boat. 'Where did you get it?'

'I made it, ma'am.'

He was a thoughtful man; this wasn't the only thing he'd done since he took up lodging at the New Liffey. The other had been to help Michael repair some of the tables in the bar room, for which he'd refused any payment.

Milligan reached into his jacket pocket and withdrew a small, wrapped parcel, which he placed on the table. 'And here is a present for you, Mrs Sampson.'

This was unexpected. 'You shouldn't have, Mr Milligan.' She glanced at Michael, who clearly thought so too. Judith unwrapped it, to find a polished brass ornament in the shape of the US flag.

Milligan smiled. 'I thought you could perhaps put it on your bar somewhere, to remind you of an American whaler who graced your shores and liked what he saw.'

This was a novelty, not an intimate present, and Michael could not object to it. 'Thank you, Mr Milligan.' Judith paused and smiled. 'Now, what shall I get you in return?'

'There's no need, really.'

There came a cry from Maeve and Judith looked over; her daughter had tears in her eyes. Judith said at once, 'What did you just do, Liam?'

'He pinched me!' Maeve said. 'On the leg.'

'Liam?' Judith said. 'Did you do that?'

Liam looked at his toy boat and didn't respond straight away. He looked at David Milligan, then back to his mother. 'She kicked me first!'

Judith said, 'Be nice to each other, because today is Jesus's birthday. He loved us all.' Maeve made a po face at her brother, who returned it with a glare. Judith laughed. 'Children!' she said as she turned to Milligan. 'Did you attend services this morning? We couldn't, of course. We Catholics don't even have a place of worship yet, but we're hoping for one.'

'I did, in fact, at Saint Philips. It's an interesting church, to say the least.'

Judith helped Maeve with the last of her dinner. 'Interesting would not be the word I'd use, Mr Milligan. To my mind the layout is terrible, and some parts of it look about to fall down.'

He smiled. 'I didn't need to keep my arms above my head for protection, Mrs Sampson.' Judith smiled at this. 'But I do see what you mean.'

'And what else would you like to do when you're in town?'

Milligan had no special plans; he reckoned that he hadn't even had the chance to explore the rest of The Rocks. As they spoke, he often had to raise his voice to be heard above the laughter surrounding their Christmas table.

* * *

David Milligan finished his breakfast and left the New Liffey at 8:45 am on 28 December, the last Sunday of 1823. He paced along Cumberland Street for the eighty-yard walk to St Philips Church near York Street. This precinct, like most of The Rocks, had no regular kerb and the house frontages were all aligned differently to the street. Its randomness of built form was much like the variety among its residents. This was a polyglot neighbourhood, where a magistrate might find himself living alongside a cobbler.

Milligan was preoccupied: all he could think of was whether he was about to see a certain young woman again. Last Thursday, at church on Christmas morning, he had spied her with her family, or so he assumed them to be. He couldn't take his eyes off her and he had felt an instant attraction, unlike any other that he'd felt. During the months or years at sea, of course he was like other men in that he missed the company of women. But when he and his shipmates came ashore, he was not as quick as they to take advantage of what was on offer. His mates were out to drown their sorrows and satisfy their physical needs, but this time, to him, Sydney didn't seem like the usual port of call.

Instead, the night before, when his friends and he had gone to a brothel in Fort Street, he'd taken a good look at what was on offer but hadn't partaken in their pleasures. Not that he didn't want to, no, it was just that he suddenly felt he needed something deeper and more fulfilling. He did not feel superior to his comrades—no, by God, he had his faults, perhaps more than many men. It was just that he liked Sydney in a different way from his mates. He recognised a strange new hankering to settle down. And the dark-eyed young brunette whom he'd seen at Christmas service had struck him as just the woman to share that new life with.

He crossed York Street and went into St Philips Church. It was Church of England, but similar to churches back home that he had attended. David was Episcopalian, so the place did not seem unfamiliar. He smiled, however, as he remembered Mrs Sampson's description of the building at her Christmas table. With a carpenter's eye, he had surveyed its structure, and he had seen that its asymmetrical layout of roof timbers was indeed poor. The masonry was patchy in places as well.

There were few in the congregation when he chose a pew, but the worshippers were still gathering. The young woman wasn't there yet. He sat back and thought about his parents in Boston and how they would have spent their Yuletide. This morning in Sydney the heat was starting to build already, and he thought how different it would be back home on a cold December night. Everybody would be indoors, either asleep or wrapped in woollens and sitting in front of a fire, trying to not think of the snow accumulating on roofs and piling against the doors.

He look around to see whether the young woman was arriving, and just as he did so, she walked down the aisle with the people he assumed to be her brother, mother and father. Their eyes met for all of two seconds, but for him it was enough to establish a connection. Then the family sat down in the third row of pews from the front.

The minister entered and commenced his service, but he might have been reciting the Declaration of Independence for all that David knew. His full attention was on the young woman. There was one time when she turned to adjust her jacket over her shoulders, and she glanced at him. He was tempted to smile, but managed not to. He tried to concentrate on the hymns and forget about her for a while, but this only lasted fifteen seconds. He wanted to meet her. But how could he? He knew little of Sydney and its occupants, but the manners and courtesies that he'd witnessed around the Sampsons' private table had shown him that the polite forms were just as necessary amongst townspeople here as they were at home. And this young woman was no doubt a cut above them by birth and upbringing.

He didn't belong in her world—he was a feckless foreign whaler who had breezed into harbour on a damaged ship and was supposed to go back on the ocean again as soon as it was repaired. He couldn't just approach her and say 'hello'. He'd need to be introduced to her family before he could speak to her. He wondered whether Mrs Sampson knew these people; if so, she might know a way for him to meet the young woman formally. But was that likely? For the rest of the service, he puzzled over ways he might approach her without being rebuffed or simply ignored by her well-dressed father and mother.

When the service ended, David stayed put, opened his Bible and read the psalms, glancing from time to time at the people coming up the aisle beside him. He saw her family starting to move and waited until they were about to pass by. He was in luck: the young woman was walking behind the rest of her family and, just as she passed him, she glanced at him again. Thrilled, he stood up and followed them outside into the bright sunshine. About ten parishioners had gathered to talk and the minister was among them. But the young woman's family did not linger, so David had no chance to stand near them and try striking up a conversation. They walked away, probably towards their home, and he trailed them at a distance down York Street, which was not busy, with just the odd horse and cart, and riders going back and forth. Keeping his distance, he followed them. They passed a stationary water cart with two men beside it, and turned down

Charlotte Place. It was a steep and narrow incline and the southern boundary of The Rocks which led towards George Street. They never turned around, so he could follow them downhill without their noticing him.

He came to halt, however, when the family were two-thirds of the way down the slope, because another young woman appeared from a house and they greeted her. The parents and brother kept on walking but the daughter lingered to talk to the friend. They had been speaking for a while when David heard a noise behind him, and turned. Water was gushing from the wagon on York Street, picking up dirt and detritus as it flowed merrily down the steep incline towards the two young women. The friends said goodbye and the other young woman went back into her house. David meanwhile was tearing down the hill, trying to outdistance the dirty flood that was about to overwhelm the feet of the young woman he had been following. She was walking on towards her family, oblivious of him and everything behind her.

'Look out!' David cried, not five feet from her.

When she turned and looked at him, the scum had nearly reached her, so he kept on going, flung his arms around her waist and lifted her away from the flowing waste. She gasped when he grabbed her, took a shocked step away when he set her down, then she looked at the brown flood that she had escaped, and started to laugh. 'That would have been a nice mess!'

She had a lovely voice, and glowing eyes to match.

'I'm sorry,' David said, 'to be so sudden. I had to move you out of the way.'

'Of course, you had to. So, I thank you, Mister ...?'

'Milligan, ma'am, I mean miss, I'm sorry. My name's David. And your name, Miss ...?'

Out of the corner of his eye, David noted that the parents were continuing to stroll downhill, oblivious, and the brown flood had petered out behind them. But the brother had seen everything, and lost no time in striding up to them. He was well-built and about

Milligan's age. He spoke to his sister but he was looking directly at David. 'Are you all right, Jane?'

'Of course; there's nothing wrong with me, thank you.' She smiled at David. 'But I might have ruined my shoes if this kind man had not acted.'

The brother gave a curt nod to David. 'Thank you. Sister, it's time we were off.'

Jane looked at David. 'My name is Jane Wilson, Mr Milligan, and thank you again. By your speech I'd say you are from the United States. Am I right?'

'Come, Jane,' the brother said, 'Father and Mother will be wondering where we are.'

Jane ignored him for the moment and said to David, 'Do you come to Saint Philips regularly?'

'Yes, Miss Wilson, I do.'

She nodded at him. 'Goodbye and thank you again.'

David watched them go, thrilled by this unexpected contact. The parents were out of sight beyond a twist in the narrow street—he didn't think they had even seen the encounter. He should not keep following, of course, now that he and his good services had been shrugged off by Jane's brother, but he had to. He had to see this attractive and charming young woman again and he did not feel like waiting until the next Sunday service to do it.

Jane Wilson was excited. As she and her brother Henry headed down towards George Street, at some distance behind her parents, she thought about the American. He was tall and strong; he'd lifted her away from the rushing water like a feather. He had lovely hair, a clear and tanned complexion, and a bright smile. She wondered what he did. His garb was simple, not tailored, but his shirt was clean and pressed.

She said to Henry, 'I suppose that man's a sailor, because he's American—but he didn't have a common way of talking. Is he some kind of tradesman, do you think?'

'No, sure to be off a ship. Probably nothing but a whaler. Whaling: that's a rough and filthy trade, if you like!'

'And important,' she said. 'It's a big thing in Sydney.'

'It's essential, I grant you. Here and around the world.'

Henry was right. Products from whaling were part of their daily life, like the whalebone corsets she and her mother wore under their best dresses. Even the oil they used to see and read at night was from the leviathan. And the trade yielded precious ambergris as well. Port Jackson was full of whaling boats and Mosman Cove, on the north side of the harbour, was a whaling station. For the rest of the way to her house, she thought about the American and found that she was looking forward to seeing him again, on the first Sunday of the new year.

When David Milligan reached George Street, there was no sign of Jane Wilson's parents, but he saw her and her brother enter a house that had a well-tended frontage on the street itself. He walked past it, looking at it sidelong and wondering if there was a way to circle to the other side of the property. About ten yards further on, he found he could turn left up a lane that linked George Street to Harrington Street and sure enough, there was another lane that ran behind the Wilson's house, garden and stables. The fence palings were new and so was the garden gate. Through a gap between the gate and the fence post he could see that the garden was lush with burgeoning plants that partly obscured the back wall and door of the house from view. When no one came out into the sunlit garden, he turned away with regret. But he knew her name and where she lived! He returned to the New Liffey, a happier man than when he had left it.

* * *

During the end of 1823 and the first three days of the new year, David was working at Cockle Bay. It was an area of patchy scrub around the inlets west of the promontory occupied by The Rocks. Along the tree-lined banks, ships were being repaired and careened. David's task, with a skeleton crew, was repairing the hole in his whaling ship, *Cyprus*. When his brain wasn't occupied with joinery, measuring, planning, and sawing, he thought about Jane Wilson. It was a unique feeling. Yes, there were girls back home who had caught his eye and others, not many, who had got to know him well. But this young woman was different.

On Sunday, 4 January, he planned to meet her alone, simply to get to know her better. In these times, young ladies—for so she would be considered by society—could only venture forth from home with a chaperone if they were single; and whether married or single, they were never supposed to walk with male strangers. David had already been snubbed by Jane's brother, which gave him little hope of getting to know her family. But he was desperate to see her alone—how else could he get to know *her*? And he had to do this soon, because he would only be in town for as long as the *Cyprus* was at Cockle Bay, and repairs on the ship's hull were going well, because he couldn't bear to do shoddy work.

His anxiety rose as the service at St Philips was ending. As he had done the previous Sunday, he was guilty of paying less attention to his God while his thoughts were on Jane Wilson. He was luckier in the outcome this time, however, because when the family left the church, they paused to talk to friends. David made his move while Jane's parents and brother were with three other people and Jane was by herself, behind another group that shielded her from her parents' view.

'Good morning, Miss Wilson.'

She looked up at him and smiled. 'Good morning to you, Mr Milligan.'

David came straight to the point. He pulled out a pamphlet from his pocket: two folded pages that contained a note he had written to her. Keeping an eye out for her parents and brother, he offered her the paper. 'I have something on Boston that you might find interesting.'

She accepted the pamphlet and opened it. 'Thank you.' The moment she saw the note, she said, 'What's this?'

At that moment her brother began walking over to her.

'Could you please read that later?' Milligan said to her in a low voice. 'It's not disrespectful, I swear.'

Jane hesitated just for a fraction, then slipped the note into her purse just as her brother came upon them.

David stood back at once. 'I bid you good day, Miss Wilson, and you, Mr Wilson.' Not waiting for a reply, David left them, hoping she would accept his humble request and be willing to meet him that evening at her garden gate. It was worth a try.

The summer sun was still light and David was in position in the lane behind the Wilson house. If Jane Wilson was in agreement, she would appear at eight o'clock. They might not have long to talk, but even a short meeting would be a miracle. If she didn't come, there could only be two reasons. One: that she could not get away to see him. Two, which was depressing: that she didn't want to see him at all. The minutes ticked by, he drew closer to the gate, then worried that he might be spotted from the house. He pulled out his watch. Eight pm precisely. Suddenly he heard rustling sounds on the other side of the fence.

He heard her voice, though he couldn't see her yet. 'Are you there, Mr Milligan?'

He murmured, 'You're here! Thank you! Could you move closer to the gate, please, Miss Wilson?'

He moved closer as well and suddenly he could see her through the gap between the fence post and the gate. A bright sliver of her, divided by the six inch metal hinges. A vignette made up of one brown eye and her smooth cheek and brow with the dark hair above, and below was the modest blue dress with a full skirt clasped around her eighteen-inch waist. 'I can spare you perhaps five minutes, Mr Milligan. I told my mother I would collect some strawberries and see that the rabbits don't get them. I did that much earlier, so we have some time now.'

'You're very good. I know this is kind of forward of me, Miss Wilson, and I should only see you with other people.'

He thought he heard a giggle at that, but her hand came up to hide her mouth. 'I'm sure this fence will preclude you from doing anything more adventurous than talking with me. Have I got your assurance that you'll stay just where you are?'

'Of course you have, Miss Wilson. Now please, tell me a little bit about yourself, if you wouldn't mind.'

She dropped her hand and shifted a little, so he could see her full lips moving as she talked. 'Well then, I was born in Putney, in England, and came out here with my parents and brother. My father is a merchant. Mainly, he buys barley and hops from the farms out west and supplies them to breweries and hotels. I am eighteen years of age, and my education has been obtained through a tutor. And you?'

'Not much I can say about my education, Miss Milligan. I'm a carpenter on board a whaling ship down at Cockle Bay, which is under repair. I've been in Sydney since just before Christmas and I like the place and I like the people, especially a young woman I've seen at Saint Philips.'

'Mr Milligan,' she said, 'you cannot say such things.'

'They may not be permissible, Miss Wilson, but I'm telling the truth and I mean no harm.'

She turned her face away and there was silence on the other side of the gate for some time. 'How long will you be in town?'

'We are part way through our repair. Finishing it could take two weeks or more.'

'And you will go back to America after that?'

'No,' he said, 'we head to the South Island of New Zealand, hunting whales again, and from there to the Hawaiian Islands, then back home.'

There was a sound of a house door opening, and Jane started. 'There is somebody coming. I'll see who it is. Wait here.' Her skirt swished against the gate as she moved away.

David side-stepped and pressed himself against the fence.

'Jane, what are you doing?' came a voice that David assumed to be her mother's.

'I'm still gathering, Mother! I'll be a few minutes yet.'

'All right, dear, but it'll soon be too dark to see what you're doing. Make sure you leave the beds rabbit-proof.' There was a pause, then the sound of the door closing.

Jane reappeared, looking a little flustered, but the brown eye looking at him through the gap still had a soft glow. 'Mr Milligan, I think I should go inside. But would you think it very forward of me if we could talk another time soon, like this?'

David was excited, and he knew she would be able to hear this in his voice. 'I would like that very much. Can I come here on Wednesday, late afternoon, about five?'

'So soon!' To David, the three days would seem like an age and he was disappointed that she didn't share the feeling—but then he realised she was simply nervous. She lowered her gaze to think, and then said, 'Very well, I'll try to be here, but if I'm not here by a quarter after the hour, please don't wait—I'll have been prevented for some reason.' There was a pause, then she said with a shy glance, 'I can leave a note under our garden toolbox, beside the gate. If you move to your right and look through the gap at your feet, you'll see the box.'

He did as she said, and bent down from the waist. Through the gap under the gate he could see Jane's neat leather shoes and the hem of her blue dress. Further to the right her fingertips appeared, pointing to the place underneath the garden toolbox. He would have loved to reach through and touch her fingers, but she withdrew them. He stood up. 'I understand. Thank you very much for seeing me and taking this risk.'

Her face appeared again beyond the hinges of the gate. He could see that she was smiling. 'America sounds a fascinating place, Mr Milligan, and I would like to know more about it. Until Wednesday afternoon, then. Goodbye.' She turned away.

'Goodbye to you, Miss Wilson.'

David's heart beat faster as he went along the lane and up to Harrington Street, towards his hotel.

On the next day, Monday 5 January, he worked into the early evening. He and his crew had spent the time squaring the jagged hole in his ship and sawing the infill timbers to length. David got a wherry boat across from Cockle Bay to the promontory, as thunder pounded from the south. A storm was due to reach the town and he was keen to get to the hotel before it hit. As he alighted at the Market Street wharf, his luck ran out and the rain fell, hitting him with pellet-like drops, and he started to run. The southerly drove the rain against him and the darkness settled in as he forged along the dimly lit street. He turned left into Sussex Street, which was even less illuminated, and deserted. However, above the din of the rain, he heard raised voices coming from somewhere on his left.

It sounded as though the conversation was turning into an argument, so he increased his pace, to avoid getting involved in any conflicts. But a bolt of lightning crashed somewhere quite close behind him, and rather than be out in the open in a thunderstorm he sought shelter under an awning over a doorway. The argument was only yards away. When there was a pause in the thunder, he had no choice but to hear what went on—an angry altercation between two men.

'You invited me here to settle this order, but I'm not placing it with you unless I'm satisfied. I'm not obliged to buy barley and hops from you, sir.'

'I'm telling you, Mr Ryan,' the other man said, 'that you will pay my price and accept my conditions.' The man laughed. 'You won't get better.'

'But I can try for that, and I certainly will.'

There was a pause. 'Try if you will, but I know the other grain suppliers, and they won't treat with you. You have a habit, Mr Ryan, of not paying for what you have contracted to buy. I had to wait three months for your money on my last sale to you. This time you will give me a bank draft.'

'I'm a man of business, just like you,' the other man replied. 'I want the best deal for me.'

'Good business doesn't mean shifty business.'

'Are you calling me dishonourable?'

'You are untrustworthy, sir. Your record tells against you. I know two suppliers who've had to get the courts onto you to pay up. I'll not have that. Now you either pay me on my terms and conditions or I won't supply you ever again.'

'You're a greedy man,' Ryan said. 'And a mean one. I know your barley and it is never one hundred per cent. No, it is not indeed. It is full of chaff. I have proof of that.'

'It is not, sir. You will retract that now. I have a reputation to protect.'

'I retract nothing. It's true, and I'll tell that truth to anyone.'

There was a pause and David strained to hear what would happen next. The voices were those of mature men and they were both in trade—surely they weren't likely to come to blows, like a pair of drunken sailors?

The trader roared, 'You'll retract your slander, now!'

There was a laugh from Ryan that turned into an angry cry. 'You struck me, sir!'

'You get what you deserve!' came the response.

David stuck his head into the downpour and looked around the corner. He could see a vacant site. To one side of this, under a canopy attached to a stable, were the two men, now engaged in punching at each other. Some of the blows were landing and others not. Both men were about middle-aged and of equal height and David saw no reason to intervene in their squabble.

He ducked his head back under the awning and looked up at the sky; maybe the storm was passing and he could move on. Then he heard a groan. He peered around again. This time, one of the men was prone on the ground, motionless in the rain, just outside the shelter of the canopy. The other man was kneeling beside him, examining him but not touching him. David had seen enough fights in his time to sense that the man lying on the ground was unconscious.

This looked serious. In an instinctive reaction, David stepped out into the street, but then stopped dead in shock—at that very instant, a bolt of lightning struck a lamppost nearby, almost deafening him, and illuminated the space between himself and the two combatants with a brutal white light.

The man on his knees looked up and saw David at once. The man glanced down at the other man on the ground, looked back at David, then leaped up and ran away. He was gone from the site in seconds, darting around to the rear of the stables—were there steps beyond, leading away from Sussex Street?

David went straight to the man on the ground. The rain was still pelting down and he'd soon be soaked to the skin, but its coolness had failed to bring the prone man into consciousness. David didn't like the way the man was lying—one arm flung out, the other caught under him, and his head at a grotesque angle beside a large stone, as though he had dashed it as he fell. There was no blood, but the man's chest was not moving. With a sense of dread David bent down and felt for the pulse at the throat. There was none. The skin was warm, but the heart and lungs had ceased to function. He was touching a corpse. The man had been killed in the fight.

David shivered and stood up. He stepped under the shelter of the canopy by the silent stables and stared at the scene. The victim was past help. The rain was creating pools on the vacant site and the atmosphere was eerie, because the split and scorched lamppost was steaming from the lightning strike. What to do?

David was a whaler, a foreign sailor in transit. Men like him were considered tough and unruly at best, and out-and-out ruffians at the worst. Fisticuffs, brawls, drunken behaviour and serious crime often brought them to the notice of the police. If David reported the murder—which he should do, since he was its only witness—there was the risk that he'd find himself the chief suspect.

He cursed and looked at the victim again. Shouldn't the man's killer be identified to the police? Then it would be up to the law to decide whether he'd been murdered, or died by misadventure. The thing was, David was fairly confident he would recognise the culprit if he saw him again, because he'd been clearly illuminated by the lightning strike, and he'd seen his figure from the back as he ran. A well-dressed, short man with a clean-shaven face. A well-to-do merchant, a grain supplier. There had been something familiar about him, too, as though David had seen him before.

He needed to know who that was, lying on the ground. Was it the man named Ryan, or was it Ryan who had dealt the fatal blow and then escaped? David dashed out into the rain again and went through the victim's pockets. He quickly found an invoice in one of the jackets, addressed to Mr Peter Ryan. There were some wax matches in another pocket, and David struck one to see the paper. The invoice was for delivery by a coal merchant, addressed to Peter Ryan. There was money and another paper in the pocket where he'd found the matches, but David was nervous about standing about by a dead body in the darkness of a deserted street. He thrust the coal invoice back in Ryan's pocket and kept the other paper to look at later. Ryan would be found and identified; David couldn't bring him back to life by reporting his death.

He stepped back to Sussex Street through the puddles on the site. The rain had lessened but he was still shivering. Was he irresponsible, letting the victor in the fight go free? Perhaps not, because what he had just witnessed was not a premeditated act, but the result of anger on both sides. A fight had ended in a death that by the laws of New South Wales might be murder, or manslaughter, or death by misadventure—David had no idea. All he knew was that fights ending like this were not uncommon in sea ports around the world. Though they seldom occurred between well-to-do men who were engaged in trade.

His first instinct was to go back to his hotel lodgings, not to the police. He set off for the New Liffey, knowing this would haunt him for days to come.

Chapter Two

The downpour that had happened overnight was typical of the heavy rains that deluged Sydney in summer. The colony was in its infancy, and Sydney's streets and roofs were not yet paved and drained as European cities were. Drenching showers and storms made the streets muddy at best and sludge at worst. In the New Liffey hotel, early the next morning, Judith Sampson was mopping up. The floor of an upstairs room was wet in one corner; she would have to get Michael to fix that part of the roof. Judith was anxious about possible leaks in the other lodgers' rooms, but when she knocked on the doors and called out to other occupants, they reassured her. She was about to knock on Milligan's door when he opened it himself and stepped out. She was surprised—he was usually gone to his work earlier than this.

He looked startled, but collected himself and murmured, 'Good morning, Mrs Sampson.'

'Good morning, Mr Milligan,' she said. 'I didn't see you come in last night. Were you all right in that deluge? And I'm just checking that you didn't get any rain in your room.'

'Yes… Yes, I mean no. No leaks, Mrs Sampson. Excuse me, I must get down to Cockle Bay. Until this evening.' With that he nodded and hurried downstairs.

Odd, thought Judith. He was normally alert and in good humour, instead of tired and grumpy. Not to worry, he might have had too many drinks the night before. She wondered where he had drunk them; not in her hotel, at any rate. She concentrated on her next Tuesday chore, changing all the bed linen.

* * *

It was Wednesday afternoon, and David was making his way along Gloucester Street towards Harrington, heading for the lane behind Jane Wilson's house.

He had not contacted the police about Ryan, and he wasn't going to. The death had been reported in the newspapers and the police had listed it as suspicious. It was impossible to tell from the reports whether they were undertaking a serious investigation but Ryan was after all a citizen of Sydney town, not a ruffian who'd gone down in a street fight, so they must be making some attempt to find out who had knocked him out and broken his neck. Should David be trying to assist them in that investigation? He wished he could talk to someone about it, because he'd worried about it for the last two days and got little sleep in consequence. Might he talk to his intelligent, approachable landlady? Well, the one person he wouldn't share this with was Jane Wilson, the woman he was longing to see.

It was ten to five and the sun was still strong as he waited behind the fence. At 4:55 he heard a cart and looked up as a tinker came along the lane towards him. David got down on one knee and pretended to do up his boot laces. The cart passed him, and he watched until it had turned out of the lane.

Jane whispered from behind the fence, 'Mr Milligan! Are you there?'

'Aye,' David said, 'it's me.'

The beautiful sliver that was all he could see of her came into view again. This time she was wearing a yellow dress, but her smile was the same. 'I am glad you came.'

'Try keeping me away. You've no idea how much I look forward to seeing you.' He gave a nervous laugh. 'Well, I can't quite see all of you, but I love hearing your voice. I could listen to you all day.'

He thought she might be blushing, and she lowered her eyes without answering, then she recovered and said, 'How is your boat going? The repair I mean.'

'It's going quite well, thank you. What did you tell your parents about being out here this afternoon? How long can we talk?'

'I've told them I'm doing a spot of weeding. So I started it about a quarter of an hour ago. Could you tell me more about America?'

David came closer. 'I've only seen a section of its eastern seaboard and the ports, especially Boston. It is very much like Sydney. Some of its buildings are of course older and more established and made of brick, which is understandable. There is a lot of our continent being opened up to the west, so the future looks good.'

'It all sounds so fascinating,' she said.

'And what about yourself, Miss Wilson? What do you do by day?'

'I read and I sew. And I help my mother with some visits to charities.'

'You are a good person.' He said it not so much because of her words as because of the soft expression in her eyes.

She looked surprised but pleased. 'Thank you. I do my bit.'

'And your father?' David said. 'You said he's a grain merchant—do you have anything to do with his business?'

She laughed. 'No, he has my brother, Henry, to train up over hops and barley. From those products the people of Sydney make all sorts of things.' She gave him a sparkling glance. 'Including beer, which perhaps you like to imbibe?'

He thought of the encounter two nights ago on a vacant lot: two grown men fighting about a transaction over grain. He must banish it from his mind. 'I suppose you get about a lot in society?'

'Henry accompanies me when we're invited to dances and the governor's balls. Other than that, life is straightforward and uneventful, Mr Milligan; unlike yours, which is filled every day with new adventures. Not only that, but you have the freedom to see the world and all that it offers. I wish I could do that.'

'If you did have the opportunity, miss, where would you want to go?'

David was met with another laugh. 'Dear me, I would never get that chance, especially on my own. I must take my solace from books and other interesting things to read. Men are so lucky that way.'

'You want to expand your mind?'

'And my experiences. Of course. Just because I'm a woman, I don't stop thinking about what I'd like to do and what I'd like to see. So, where should I go first—in my mind, if not in reality?'

She wasn't like the girls he knew back home; the ones he knew as a youth seemed content with being domesticated. Her attractions for him were more than physical; he was responding to her inquisitive mind. 'There's the islands in the South Pacific, which you would find fascinating.'

He saw a moment of regret in her eye and she said in a quiet, almost sad tone, 'Alas, Mr Milligan, my life right now is filled by books, and they can only expand my imagination. Now, that's quite enough about me. Where are your lodgings—on ship or on shore?'

'I have a room at the New Liffey hotel.'

'Oh, in Cumberland Street. Yes, I know it. I believe the landlady and licensee is a woman?'

'Mrs Sampson,' David said. 'Though she and her husband seem to be equal partners in the enterprise.'

'I think that should be all for now, Mr Milligan. Unfortunately, I need to resume my weeding. Boring though it is. Nonetheless, I've enjoyed our conversation.'

It seemed abrupt. He examined her face to catch her expression, but her eyes were lowered. He said, 'As you wish. Shall I see you after service this Sunday?'

She murmured, 'I would like that very much.'

His heart lightened a little. 'Thank you, Miss Wilson. Perhaps you might think of a way for us to talk together in the presence of your parents, without attracting censure for your conduct.'

There was a pause, and David thought he'd overstepped the mark, but she said. 'That's an interesting problem to solve. I shall put my mind to it. Goodbye, Mr Milligan.'

David walked off, rapt in the picture of her that he took away, and the soft sound of her voice.

Three boys, their patched pants and shirts indicative of the poor denizens of The Rocks, were tearing down the lane towards him.

David smiled at the youngsters' simple lives. He went to grab one in jest and was greeted by an oath that would have made a sailor proud.

He continued on his way. Jane Wilson had already led him far down the road of attraction. David Milligan was falling in love.

* * *

The comings and goings in the New Liffey in the next three days went without undue incident. On Saturday night, during a break in the busy evening, Michael Sampson looked up from reading from the *Gazette*. 'They're still looking for whoever downed Peter Ryan. It's been nearly a week now and they haven't laid hands on anyone for it.'

'Ryan?' Judith said next to him. 'Do we know him? I don't think he's ever been in here. Either to drink our beer, or sell us his barley.'

'No, I've never sold him a glassful or bought from him. But he died not far from here, just off Sussex Street. On the night of the storm.'

There was the sound of glass breaking and both husband and wife looked up. David Milligan, sitting at the table nearest to them, said, 'Sorry, Mrs Sampson. That was clumsy and I'll pay for it.'

'No need,' Michael Sampson said, eyeing his lodger. Milligan was a calm fellow most evenings, but tonight he seemed on edge.

'Get me a broom and a mop, please,' Milligan said, 'and I'll clear it up. It's the least I can do.'

Michael Sampson nodded. 'Good. Behind me, down the corridor, you'll find a cupboard with what you need. And thank you.'

Judith looked about to get up and fetch the broom but Michael frowned at her—she was too good to the customers sometimes, jumping at their whim. It would do them good to see their landlady taking it easy for a change. He looked around and it was still quiet, so he continued to read the newspaper. 'Hang on: Peter Ryan. He did sell to us, just the once, at the beginning of last year, Judith, do you remember? His hops were poor quality. Yes of course, I remember now.'

'Not the best merchant, yet he didn't deserve to die, for all that. Such a shame. If he met his end just down the hill, I wonder the coppers haven't been around questioning whether he was up this way on the night.'

Michael shrugged. 'Plenty of other public houses he might have frequented. Sydney's not short of pubs.'

Later that evening, as Judith, Michael and the staff were cleaning up after the hotel closed, David Milligan was still seated at his table. Judith noticed that he had been quiet all evening since the broken glass incident, and she sensed there was something on his mind. Every day she felt that something like friendship was growing between the young whaler and herself; and she thought, just for a moment, about the regret she would feel when he had to leave Sydney. She would talk with him.

She said in a low voice to Michael, 'Love, are we just about finished in here?'

Michael looked around and nodded. 'Pretty much.'

'Would you mind if I have a few words with our lodger? I've got the feeling things are not quite well with him, and he's got nobody else to talk to.'

Michael reached over and squeezed her elbow. 'You're a good woman, Mrs Sampson.'

Judith smiled at him, left the bar and took a seat at the table of her lodger. 'Mr Milligan.'

He looked at her with a strained expression and she could see that there was something really worrying him. 'Mrs Sampson, could I ask for a big favour: that you call me David? There's not much difference between our ages and …' He gave a helpless grin. 'Gee, I know it's not the done thing, but I'll be off your hands soon. Would you mind?'

Judith didn't mind at all. In fact, she welcomed it. She leaned forward, though not in an intimate way, and said with a smile, 'And you can call me Judith when no one else is around.' They both relaxed and Judith was glad of the change in him. But his grim expression returned. 'What is wrong? Please tell me.'

'There are two things on my mind. Both of which I find difficult to solve, or at least work through to some point where I'll be satisfied.'

'Go on,' she said.

David Milligan exhaled, and it seemed to Judith that he was glad that he was finally confiding in someone. 'I've met a young woman to whom I'm attracted.'

Judith sat back, careful to hide her surprise. She had to admit, she had been thinking that Milligan had perhaps had thoughts about herself, even though she was married. He was a good-looking young man and free to see whomever he liked. The mere thought made her feel a little silly—of course, it was natural that he would find young women more attractive than his landlady ... 'And does she return your feelings?'

Milligan nodded. 'It's early days but I think she does. This sounds daft I know, Judith, but because I'm only in Sydney for a short time I want to make things go faster between us, if you know what I mean.' He looked at her in an earnest way. 'And I don't mean anything disreputable by that. I swear, she's the sort of woman that I'd wish for as a wife, not for anything else.'

Judith nodded, glad he wasn't sharing confidences with her about a street woman. She often had to shoo out prostitutes who wandered into the hotel every now and again, looking for inebriated patrons. There were enough around the Rocks and Judith knew where they plied their trade. She didn't want them in the New Liffey but she wasn't moralistic; in fact she helped them where she could with spare food from the pub, and a coin or two given here and there.

She readjusted her ideas and concentrated on what David Milligan was saying. Against all probability he was looking for a wife in Sydney, and that could be considered good, for a whole lot of reasons. 'Have you met her many times?'

'I have seen her in public but of course without an introduction, we cannot converse. Please don't get me wrong. All our dealings so far have been above board and she is a young lady of repute.'

Judith smiled. 'I'm sure she is.' But she thought a note of reality could be introduced at this point. 'However, you should not prejudice that reputation by meeting in an underhand way. It's not fair on her.'

'Of course, I don't want to do that. However, she's seeing me by her free choice. She is forthright in her opinions and she's trying to decide what to do with her life. Her speech is eloquent and educated and she is attractive ... like yourself.'

'You are free with your compliments, David.' Judith was both intrigued and little envious of this new woman in David's life. She sounded amazing, with her forceful needs and wants; and she showed courage by talking to David, who was, after all, just a carpenter working on a whaling ship. Judith was not being elitist. She never forgot that she herself had been a spinner back in Dublin: one of the lower classes.

David said, 'I want to make sure I don't compromise the young lady. In due course, if things work out the way we both want—and I think they will—I shall make overtures to her father.' He smiled at Judith. 'Perhaps that could be done in the presence, or with the knowledge of, two of the leading publicans around town, Mr and Mrs Michael Sampson?'

Judith laughed at his cheek, then shook her head slightly. 'Easier said than done, but if things work out between the two of you, then I'll do my best to advise. Now, is that all that's been troubling you?'

'No, it isn't.' He paused. 'I was a witness to a man dying in a fight. It was last Monday night, during the storm. It happened on my way back to the hotel.'

Judith was shocked. 'No! Where?'

'In Sussex Street, not far from Market Street. The man who died was Peter Ryan.'

Judith gasped. 'Good heavens, don't tell me you were involved?'

David gave a bitter smile. 'That's a good question, and one most people would ask, given that I'm a common seaman. But no. I was exhausted after a long day at work, trying to make my way back here through the storm, and I heard the fight but didn't see it. I saw the result: one man dead on the ground, the other getting up and running away.'

Judith believed him; he had a haunted look in his eyes, as though he remembered every moment. 'Did you go to the police?'

'No.'

'Why not?'

'More than one reason. First, if you're the person who finds a body, the police tend to suspect you of the crime, especially if they can't find anyone else to pin it on. I could be arrested and charged with no one to defend me. Two, the man who killed Ryan saw my face. He would know me again. If the police go after him, he'll find out who's bearing witness against him, and he might get me finished off before he goes to trial. I'm the sole witness—if I can't identify him in court, how can they convict him?'

'Did you recognise him?'

'No, how could I? Whom do I know in Sydney? From the argument I heard, I know he was a trader, like Ryan, but nothing else.'

Judith said, 'They wrote in the newspaper that Ryan died of a broken neck. Are you saying Ryan's death was deliberate, or an accident?'

'I'm not saying anything. I didn't see it. I just saw the corpse.'

'Whichever,' Judith said, 'don't you feel you should go to the police, for the sake of justice?'

'That's my conundrum,' David said. 'Can I risk being nailed as a suspect? I don't see what good that would that do.'

Judith held his eye. 'Then tell me more. You need to talk to *someone*. Talk to me.'

'All right. I overheard the whole argument because I was near to both men, sheltering out of the rain. There was fault on both sides, I can swear to that. I got the feeling both traders might be engaged in underhand practices. Ryan got hit first, then they both started swinging punches. The perpetrator must have landed a devastating one, because I heard Ryan groan. Either the blow killed him outright, or he knocked his head when he fell. I stepped out a couple of seconds later, the attacker got a good look at me, and he fled.' David gave her a beseeching look. 'What was I to do? The whole thing was over in minutes. What would you have done?'

She hesitated. On the spot, she found it a very hard question to answer. 'Let me think on it for you.'

He looked nervous. 'You won't tell anyone else?'

She shook her head. 'No, you've told me this in confidence and I respect that. But Peter Ryan had a wife who depended on him and if I were her I'd be desperate for justice. She'll be giving the police her help, you can be sure. I'd say, let the police do their work, and see what comes of it. If they reach a dead end, and you find the whole thing is still preying on your mind, then you might decide to take action after all. Or you might not. In the meantime, I'll find out what stories are going around about Peter Ryan's death, and maybe the truth will be uncovered, without your lifting a finger.' She smiled at him.

He smiled back. 'You're a good woman, Judith. Thank you.'

* * *

All the next week was uneventful, as Judith went about her normal duties in her hotel. On Friday 16 January, one of her barmen came up to her. 'Missus, there's two constables who want to talk to you. They're outside.'

It was half an hour before the hotel was due to open, but Judith went at once to the front door. Like the average person in The Rocks, she was wary of the police, and indeed of anyone in authority. This attitude was ingrained in her because of her humble upbringing in Dublin, and it had not changed when she was transported to Sydney. She was suspicious of those in the top strata of society and she knew that the ones with power used it to their own advantage, and against the little people. The police belonged amongst the little people themselves, but they too had a power of their own, that they used at will and often without any consistency or fairness. Still, she had a job to do keeping the peace in her hotel, and she had to admit her life would be harder if the police weren't doing the same in the streets. The least she could do was give them a hearing. She unbolted the front door.

'Good morning,' she said. 'Can I help you?'

The taller of the two constables took off his helmet. 'I'm Constable Martin, madam, and this is Constable Walsh.' The smaller constable nodded. 'We're making enquiries about the death of Mr Peter Ryan in Sussex Street last Monday night. This hotel is a fair way from the crime scene, but we've been working our way through the public houses in The Rocks to see whether anyone noticed Ryan's movements that night. Did you see him here, or has anyone here mentioned him, either last week or since?'

'There's been talk, of course. I hear patrons mention Ryan now and then but most of it sounds like gossip to me.' Judith was telling the truth, here; as she'd promised David Milligan, she had been listening for details at the bar-room tables, but the cause of death remained a mystery and the newspapers had thrown no new light on the death either. She went on, 'I mean, no one seems to know whether it was murder or some sort of accident. Can you tell me that, Constable?'

'We cannot share any of the investigation with you, Mrs Sampson, but we do think someone else might have been involved.' He put on his helmet. 'Consequently, if you hear anything that might give us a lead, please report to The Rocks police station, down the hill. Good morning.'

Judith nodded. 'Good morning to you.'

She went back inside and walked through the public rooms, checking that all was ready for opening time. But she was thinking about David Milligan. The police believed someone else was involved—that meant they'd found signs of a fight when they examined the body and the surroundings. Could anyone place David there on the night? If they could, the longer he left to tell them his story, the guiltier he would look.

Death on the Rocks

* * *

On Sunday 18 January, David Milligan was in his usual position at service at St Philips. It was just about ready to start, and Jane Wilson wasn't there. He was disappointed. The previous Sunday, the family had attended; they'd been without the father, but David had had no opportunity to talk to Jane alone. Today, just when he'd resigned himself to not seeing her, she walked right past him together with her mother. Just the two of them, and it gave him hope.

After the service had ended, David went outside and found Jane talking with another young woman while her mother, ten feet away, was in conversation with the minister. David circled the crowd and made sure that Jane saw him. She said her goodbyes to her companion and walked his way, but not directly to him. She passed him within just the right distance for him to hear her murmur, 'See me in half an hour, in the lane.' David was pleased.

Twenty-five minutes later, he was at the back fence of her house. It was a hot day, with the temperature near one hundred, and David was mopping perspiration from his brow. He heard footsteps approaching the back fence and his anticipation rose. 'Good morning, Miss Wilson.'

'And to you, Mr Milligan,' she said. 'And how have you been this past week? Is the repair advancing to your satisfaction?'

'It is, Miss Wilson, thank you.' he said. 'I hope your family's well? There were just the two of you this morning at service.'

'My father has gone to Toongabbie. He left, when was it exactly, yes that's right, last Tuesday—yes, just after that storm we had.'

David shivered at the thought of the storm and what he had seen. He ventured, 'And your brother?'

'He accompanied my father and they both get back tomorrow. You see, my brother Henry will probably follow in my father's footsteps. So he needs to learn all about operating as a barley and hops wholesaler.'

'Ah,' David said. The two traders' angry words ran through his mind. Jane Wilson's father was in the same line of trade as Ryan and

40

the man who had caused Ryan's death—in fact he probably knew them both. This had been an unsettling thought in David's mind for some time, and today it felt horrible.

'You're silent, Mr Milligan,' Jane said. 'Is there something that concerns you? If so, please tell me.'

It was impossible to tell her what was disturbing him. 'I find my work a burden sometimes, miss, that's all. Nothing I should worry you with. How have you spent your week?'

'I've done nothing much out of the ordinary, Mr Milligan. I've done some work for Saint Philips, collecting blankets and clothes for people in need. I'm to visit Parramatta next week, to help someone in the family.'

He couldn't keep disappointment out of his voice. 'Will you be away long?'

'About five days. I'll be staying with an aunt, who is quite ill just now. She lives by herself and she really needs someone close to look after her for a while. I feel it's my duty to ease her suffering if I can.'

'You are indeed a good person, Miss Wilson.'

'I do no more than any good Christian would do, Mr Milligan. Now, tell me a little about your family.'

'I have a brother and two sisters. All of them are married and I have two nephews.'

'And the ages of your nephews?'

'Three and five, I think.' David laughed. 'By the time I get back to the US of A, they will probably be as tall I. And a sight more sophisticated.'

'No, Mr Milligan, you sound like a man of education.' Jane moved closer and her dark eye gave him an earnest look. 'I compliment you on your tone of voice and the way you express yourself. Where did you learn to speak this way?'

'My mother set the standard for our education and I'm glad she did. But it gave me a curiosity about the world that made me want to travel, instead of doing higher studies. I fell out with my father over that: he wanted me to stay home and work in his business.'

'And what business is that?'

'He has property and he's a successful tobacco grower. My two brothers were already helping him run it, and my father wanted me to train as an accountant and keep the books.'

There was a laugh from Miss Wilson. 'Dear me, and here you are on a whaling voyage, far removed from desks and dusty files and pages of numbers. The contrast is amazing! So you turned your back on college to work with your hands. You love the sea that much?'

'Yes, I do love the sea, Miss Wilson. Because it takes me to distant lands, to witness the cultures, climes, and characteristics of many nations. That's why I swapped higher education for a trade, and became a carpenter. I figured that, if all else failed in my wanderings around the globe, I could fall back on a trade that was sacred to our Lord. I have a livelihood, anywhere on earth. Right now I ply it on the *Cyprus*. Who knows where I'll practise it next?'

Jane looked away, and he could see her profile against the colourful garden beyond. He wondered whether she had realised where his conversation was headed, but was too demure to show it. She took a breath and turned back to him, her gaze bright. 'You do intrigue me, Mr Milligan, with what you can say about the world. I could talk to you all day about your travels.' He was about to reply when she went on in a more hurried fashion, 'Unfortunately, I cannot.'

He started. 'Oh, why not?' Had her parents discovered that they were meeting? Was she forbidden to see him from now on?

'That is, I won't have time in the next few days—there is so much to do before I go away. You remember, I'm going to stay with my aunt?'

He nodded, crestfallen.

'But I have a suggestion. As I said, I shall be at Parramatta for at least five days. Would you consider writing to me while I'm there? In your letters, you could tell me as much as you choose of your travels in the lands you've visited.'

'I'd consider it a privilege! What a wonderful task you put before me.' He grinned at her. 'I can promise you the most generous information, conveyed in the politest and best-chosen words.'

She giggled. 'Good. I should expect no less. The mail to Parramatta takes two days. Please take that into account and write to me early.'

David decided at once that he would write to her so that she received the first letter on her first day at her aunt's. A secret correspondence! Then he was struck by a moment's doubt. Judith Sampson had warned him not to compromise the young woman's reputation.

'But how will you explain to your aunt that you're receiving letters?'

'Oh, I have a friend in The Rocks—I shall say they're from her.'

He said at once, 'Then you can answer me, with the same excuse! Tell me you will.'

She giggled again. 'I shall definitely return your correspondence, sir, as long as yours is properly phrased.' There was a pause and then David saw a note appear through the gap between the gate and the fence. 'This is the address of my aunt.'

He was delighted that keeping in touch with him was so important to her. 'Thank you. It means a lot to me. When do you leave Sydney?'

'Next Tuesday. My brother Henry escorts me. I shall be away from the twentieth to about the twenty-fifth of this month, and perhaps a few days more.'

David held her note to his face and smelled its fragrance, a mixture of lemon and lavender. He would treasure it. 'Then,' he said, 'until you see my name in writing, Miss Wilson, I shall take my leave.' He put his fingers through the gap and was thrilled when he felt her touch them, just for an instant.

'I shall look forward to your letter, Mr Milligan,' she said. 'Very much.'

'Jane,' another voice said. 'To whom are you talking?'

David was alarmed; it must be her mother.

'I'm coming, Mother,' Jane said in a loud voice, then almost whispered, 'Goodbye Mr Milligan.'

Jane came upon her mother in the middle of their back yard. She had hoped to get further away from the gate, before Anne Wilson could glimpse David Milligan in the back lane, but the expression on her mother's face as she glared across the garden told her that their secret meeting had been discovered. Out of the corner of her eye, Jane saw David's shadow move away down the lane.

Anne Wilson said, loud enough to be heard to the fence line: 'I have something to say to you, Jane, and I want no argument. But it's hot out here. We will continue this conversation indoors.'

Jane was in trouble, and she knew there would be repercussions. She followed her mother along the twenty-yard pathway from the back fence, through a garden so lush, green and sweet-smelling that, in more pleasant circumstances, she would find it as enjoyable as ever. But she wasn't in pleasant circumstances.

The pair went through the house and into the parlour, where Mrs Wilson closed the doors to the room. She stood with her back erect. 'This is most irregular, Jane. I am very disappointed—even more, I am *alarmed* that my daughter has seen fit to be in company with a man unchaperoned.'

'I wasn't *with* him. I was just talking—'

'Nor,' Anne Wilson continued, 'has he been introduced to us!' Jane Wilson was going to say something, but her mother put her hand up. 'I don't care what his circumstances may be, he cannot see my daughter without your father and myself approving him first.'

'Mother,' Jane Wilson said, 'There wasn't a word of our conversation that you could disapprove of. Mr Milligan was talking to me about America, and—'

Her mother's eyes rounded. 'He is an American!'

'Yes, Mother. He is a carpenter on a whaling ship, *Cyprus*, currently docked in Cockle Bay.'

'A *seaman*? I'm horrified that this has occurred, and I want your word that you will not attempt to see him again.'

'But Mother,' Jane said. 'There was nothing untoward about our meetings!'

'Meetings! You mean there's been more than one? I'm appalled. I shall inform your father about what you have done when he returns from Toongabbie. After that, we can only be glad that you're going to your aunt's and away from town.'

* * *

David was upset for Jane's sake and his own that her mother had come upon them at their last meeting. He hoped the parents were not making her miserable over the indiscretion—but there was nothing he could do to help her. He had promised not to see her before she went to Parramatta, so he concentrated on the work on the *Cyprus* and wrote Jane Wilson a letter, timed so that it would arrive on her first day at her aunt's. In the letter he gave some more details about his life and his family, and ended with four questions that she could answer about herself. He posted it, and hoped that at least their correspondence would be safe from her parents' prying eyes.

At eight pm that night he left his room and went downstairs to the bar. There was a chair vacant at a table in the corner where the gamblers lived. David approached the table and looked around at the poker players, who nodded to him. He hadn't played with these men before but he took that as an invitation and sat down. They played four hands and David happened to win them all. They were about to start another when one of the men spoke up. He was about David's own height but more bulked up in the shoulders.

The man said, 'You have a habit of winning easily, Mister.'

David smiled. 'It's just my run of luck tonight. It might be your turn tomorrow night.'

The man gave him a filthy look. 'I don't think it's luck, my friend. I think you have a few tricks up your sleeve.'

David put his winnings in his pocket and gave the man a hard stare. The fellow was drunk and he was losing money, and that wasn't a good combination, especially if the man had an evil temper, which it seemed he did. 'I take an interest in the cards now and then but it's not a habit. And I don't cheat.'

The other occupants of the table were looking warily at both men. People around them shifted their chairs back, sensing a fight was in the offing.

'I am calling you a cheat,' the offended man said. 'A bloody big cheat.' He stood up flung the dregs of his beer glass over David.

Willing himself to stay collected, David looked down at his wet chest and then up at the man who was standing on the other side of the table. Then he got to his feet. At that moment, he felt a hand on his shoulder.

Michael Sampson spoke from behind him, directing his firm voice across the table. 'That's enough, Jack. I'm asking you to leave. Before you do, you'll put down a coin, to pay for this man's shirt to be washed.'

Jack looked at Sampson and David and snarled, 'You're sticking together, are you? Landlord and lodger, in each other's pockets.'

Michael Sampson didn't waste any words; he let go of David's shoulder and moved towards the other man.

Jack put his hands up. 'I'm going. I am going. Keep your shirts on, both of you.' He slapped a coin onto the table, stepped away and left the hotel.

David had had enough for one evening. With no desire to talk to Sampson or anyone else, he headed for the stairs to return to his room.

But Judith Sampson intercepted him. 'Change that shirt and bring it down to me, now. It'll stink otherwise.'

'That I'll do, Judith, thank you.' David went to his room, changed into a fresh shirt and took the other back downstairs to the scullery.

Judith was waiting for him. She accepted the shirt and shook her head at his grim face. 'Don't worry about Jack Prendergast. He's always been a pain in the you know where. We keep our eye on him. Just one more fight and we'll ban him from the New Liffey.'

* * *

For the next three days, David was working with his crew on the ship's repair. They had cut the timbers to length and fixed two long planks across the opening. Each plank measured eight inches in depth and four inches in width, and was shaped with a protruding 'tongue' on one side and a groove on the other, so that each would fit into its neighbour. They now had to fix the other two planks into position.

David's four-man team of labourers and tradesmen worked together well, except for Colin Smith, a small, wiry man with bright red hair. Smith was a carpenter like David, but lacked David's ability to plan, measure and execute complicated projects. During the last leg of their whaling voyage from the south coast, the *Cyprus*'s captain had promoted David to chief carpenter-mechanic, and the quick tempered Colin Smith had been envious of him ever since.

'Bring that over here,' David said, pointing to the next plank, which was near six feet long and made of iron. The timber was so heavy it took three men to lift it.

Smith and one of the labourers heaved up one end and a strong labourer took the other.

'Keep a good grip,' David said, though he was confident the plank would not slip out of the men's hands. They had dressed the timbers, but because the planks were part of the hull they didn't need to be baby-bottom smooth.

All at once, Smith flung out one hand, letting go of the plank and leaving the startled labourers to take the weight. It was too much and the timber smashed down onto the wharf, catching the foot of the labourer who had been paired with Smith. The man collapsed in agony, the timber came to rest beside him and meanwhile Smith was howling and waving his hand about.

'What the hell?' David yelled at Smith.

'A splinter, a bleeding splinter,' Smith shouted.

David went at once to the labourer and bent over to inspect the injury. He pulled up the trouser leg to see a painful graze on one side and swelling at the ankle.

'Not broken, by the looks of it, but you'll be badly bruised. Let's see: can you stand?' David helped the man up. He could use the leg, but only just. 'You'll see the surgeon, take the rest of the day off and keep the foot raised.'

The injured man glowered at Smith. 'You should have held onto that, not dropped it, you daft git!'

'I couldn't help it,' Smith said, 'I'm injured myself! I'm going to the infirmary to get this hand seen to.'

David inspected the splinter wound; it was just a scratch and the blood was already congealing. 'Surgeon be damned—just put a clean rag over it.'

Smith said, 'I've got to get it tended.'

David said, 'You'll stay here and finish this job.'

Smith was four inches shorter than David but he still faced up to him, his brow creased in a scowl and his eyes menacing. 'Milligan, you got no right to be high and mighty. I'm going to the surgeon and that's it. You can't stop me.'

David was going to grab the man when a voice behind him said, 'Milligan!' It was the quartermaster. 'What's the problem here?'

Smith spoke up. 'I've cut my hand, sir, and this man won't let me get it fixed.'

'He doesn't need the surgeon,' David said, then pointed to the injured labourer. 'But this man does, because of Smith's carelessness.'

The quartermaster glowered at the two workers. 'Go to the surgeon, both of you, and get fixed up.' He ran his eye over the scene. 'And you, Milligan, I want more work done today. No more stoppages, understand?'

David watched as Smith had walked away. 'Yes, sir. As long as you can assign me another man until Smith comes back.'

The quartermaster nodded. 'Meanwhile you can do what I came for—you're ordered to report to the captain. Now.'

'Aye, aye, sir.' David went aft and below decks to the captain's cabin. He knocked and entered. The man he addressed was a big man, barrel-chested and tall. The crew liked Captain Tecumseh Bates, who was known as a fair man. But why had he summoned David?

'Ah, Milligan, good,' Bates said, reaching for a ledger on his desk. 'Do you like Sydney?'

With a touch of wariness, David said, 'I do, sir.'

'Then you'll be pleased to be staying a wee bit longer. The whaling store over at Mosman Cove has need of a skilled carpenter. He has to know our industry well and be good at supervision. I've recommended you for an unspecified period. It could be weeks before you rejoin the *Cyprus*, but we'll still be here in six weeks anyway.' He handed David two sheets of paper. 'Study that. You'll find all your tasks set out. Essentially, they want three more supply rooms, which will be built from stone, so you'll be supervising masons as well. Nothing you can't handle, I'm sure. If you accept the transfer, you can report to Mosman tomorrow.'

'The repair's nearly done, sir. Then it needs at least two days for caulking and tarring. I'd like to get the timbers in before I go to Mosman Bay.'

'Granted. Who'll lead your team in your absence?'

'I'd suggest the bosun, sir, to keep an eye on them. The team's got the skills but they need telling how to approach their tasks.'

Bates opened the ledger under his hand and leafed through. He looked at David. 'Smith is an experienced carpenter. Can't he lead?' He smiled. 'He'd have been given chief carpenter not long ago, if you hadn't been aboard.'

David didn't want to criticise the man too much, but he had to give the facts. 'Smith is a good chippy, sir but he's not a leader.'

The captain looked at him for some time. 'I'll back your call, Milligan. The next task is stepping a new mizzen mast. I'll get the bosun's team onto that and Smith can pitch in; we'll see how he goes. All right, report to Mosman Cove in two days. You will be provided lodgings there but you can come back to Sydney at the end of each week if you choose. As far as the company is concerned, you're still signed up on the crew of the *Cyprus* but I'm giving you unpaid leave. I expect good behaviour from you during that leave. That will be all.'

'Aye, aye, sir,' David said. He turned and left the cabin, thrilled at the prospect of not having to leave Sydney for weeks.

Back at work, fitting the last two planks into the hull, David forced Smith to do his share of the task, alongside the replacement labourer. Smith was a troublemaker and always would be, but David had to find a way to deal with men like that, on shore and at sea, if he aimed for advancement in his trade. Might the job at Mosman Cove be a stepping stone to something bigger?

Chapter Three

It was located twenty miles west of Sydney town, but to Thomas Wilson, Toongabbie felt like the country proper. For as far as the eye could see, there was land under cultivation supplying barley, oats, wheat, sorghum and corn for the growing population of the colony's capital. It was 22 January 1824, a blistering hot day that made him glad of his broad-brimmed hat. The bare-headed farmer beside him, on the other hand, seemed unfazed by the heat and flies constantly settled on his sunburned face. Yes, Thomas Wilson liked the land, and he liked the spaciousness and the fresh air that he breathed, compared to the filth of the city.

Yet he was worried. Ever since Peter Ryan's death, his sleep had been restless and he'd had nightmares. Toongabbie usually felt like an escape and in normal circumstances he enjoyed evaluating the crops of barley, hops and oats that he would purchase. Also, he was comfortable with the banter between the farmers and the country folk. At the same time, he had a reputation as a hard man: his ruthlessness in dealing with suppliers and farmers was renowned. He had no regrets about this because he saw no reason why there should be any altruism or compassion in any of his business dealings, and he kept the nicer, gentler emotions for his relationship with his wife and his children. In his view, thoroughly nice men took holy orders. Nice men with intelligence might become teachers, maybe even lawyers. But men like himself, tough enough to survive and compete and build wealth in this burgeoning colony, belonged in trade.

Thomas Wilson had never censured himself about his own behaviour in public life, but for the past two weeks, he had had dark thoughts about his conduct on the night when Ryan died, because he had caused him to die, and whether the law would call it death by misadventure, or manslaughter, or murder, was beside the point. He was responsible and it felt like murder to him. Driving a bargain with a man, getting angry with him, even fighting him, was one thing—murder was quite another. When he'd got into that fight with Peter Ryan, yes, he'd felt loathing for the man and he'd wanted to inflict damage on him. He'd been in such a rage that he'd landed the first blow, and he had to admit that to himself. But murder—that had not been on his mind. The tragedy was that his last punch had knocked Ryan off his feet and the man had hit his head as he fell, and broken his neck. For the last fourteen days, Thomas Wilson had seen those separate moments repeating themselves in his head: Ryan going down. Ryan lying dead on the wet ground.

'Have you seen enough, Mr Wilson?' the farmer said.

Wilson concentrated on the handful of grain that he'd been inspecting. 'I want to see what you've stored in the rear of your shed. Not just the stuff that you think I need to see. I want a look at it now.'

'I'll show it to you,' the farmer said. Wilson went with him but his thoughts returned at once to the same scene and the same anguish. He was forced to live with the fact that he had caused another man's death. What made it even worse was that he had been seen by someone else as he knelt in the dirt by Ryan's body. In memory, he cursed that bolt of lightning again and again. Under that bedevilled illumination, a young man had appeared on Sussex Street and stopped right there in the rain and looked at him. Who was he? And what had he done, once Thomas got up and ran? Had he gone to the police with a description of Thomas and offered himself as a witness to murder?

There were so many complications to consider, so many risks. Left alone with the body, the young man was likely to have gone up to Ryan to at least see whether he was alive or dead. Then he might have looked in Ryan's pockets for identification. Thomas Wilson felt sick when he thought of that possibility. He had written Ryan a note to invite the man to the meeting that evening—what if Ryan had kept that note on his person, and it was now in the possession of the young man or, worse, the police? These questions and many others tormented him.

When they arrived at the rear of the shed, without a word Thomas took the farmer's shovel, dug into a pile of oats and had a look at what he found beneath the surface. When he had done this with the rest of the piles, he handed the tool back to the farmer.

'This will do me. I want all of it in sacks and on my wagons in two days. I leave the day after, to get back to Sydney for Foundation Day.'

The farmer nodded. 'It will be done.'

'And before I set out, I'll be testing a few bags at random, to make sure I've bought what I see right now before me.'

The farmer took a deep breath and exhaled. Thomas sensed his irritation: often farmers would place poor grain in the bottom of the bags and good stuff on the top, but if this farmer had fancied cheating the buyer, he was thwarted this time.

'Sure,' the man said.

When Wilson returned to his inn in the late afternoon, he was handed a letter from Sydney, in his wife's hand: a small pleasure to enjoy later. Following a bath and a full meal, he settled on the bed in his room and opened it. Blood transfused his face and he got up and paced the room.

His daughter had been seeing a man without their permission, a complete unknown who had not been introduced to the family. How dare she! She might have prejudiced her marriage prospects in Sydney society, perhaps mortally. She had had assignations with an American whaler, for goodness' sake. A whaler who lodged at the New Liffey hotel!

His wife had done the sensible thing and packed Jane off to Anne's invalid sister in Parramatta for a spell, but she would be back in Sydney by the time he got home. Good. In three days, he would confront his daughter with her indiscretions and sort her out.

* * *

On Tuesday, the day following Foundation Day, David Milligan and his crew at Mosman had just finished the setting out for the new storerooms at Mosman Cove. It was ten o'clock and he was seated under a tree drinking a mug of tea. The sky was cloudless as he gazed across the harbour, and he marvelled at how small Sydney town looked against the backdrop of the bush that surrounded it. His gaze swept across the waterfront, from Port Phillip on the western promontory, to Fort Macquarie on the left of Sydney Cove and The Rocks on the right. Among the clustered rooftops he could see grander buildings designed by a convict architect called Greenway: the governor's stables, convict barracks and St James's church, which he recognised by its spire. In the midst of it all was George Street, running down to the shoreline. He thought about the shopfronts and businesses and residences lining that street. Amongst them, near the water and below The Rocks, was the house where Jane Wilson lived.

She would be home soon. He had written to her in Parramatta, and received one reply, which he kept in his pocket. If he had written back to her at her aunt's, there was no certainty that she would have got the letter safely before having to leave for Sydney again, so on Sunday evening he'd left his message underneath the toolbox near her back gate, as they'd previously arranged. The note told her the exciting news that he would be in Sydney for some time longer, supervising construction works at Mosman Cove. He implored her to have confidence in him and keep up their friendship, because he was determined to convince her parents that he was a worthwhile man for her to see.

David Milligan acknowledged that there were challenges in his future, but he'd take them all on for the sake of Jane Wilson. He threw his tea dregs on the ground, went back onto the site and rousted up his team.

* * *

That night on the other side of the harbour, Jane Wilson was facing her father and mother in the front parlour on George Street. Thomas

Wilson's face was red with anger, and perspiration filmed his forehead and neck.

'You have probably ruined your reputation,' he said. 'This is a small town and we are a prominent family. You might have thought you were discreet but believe me, neighbours still see and hear what's going on around them and have great delight in spreading gossip.' He looked at his wife. 'No one else gave you a hint of this scandal, dear?'

'No one, Thomas,' Anne said. 'It was by sheer accident that I came out and discovered Jane lurking at the back gate with a stranger.'

Jane wasn't going down without a fight. 'He's been to worship at Saint Philips, so he's not a stranger. We've met in public, on a Sunday, what's more, and in front of people from the parish. Yes, I have talked with him alone, but every time I've had the protection and safety of our own fence. Goodness gracious, it's all innocent.'

'Innocent!' Thomas Wilson spluttered. 'It is not; it's scandalous. Dear me, an American sailor, a whaler whose reputation precedes him. I don't understand you, Jane, not at all. Where's your maidenly caution?'

'What do you mean, his reputation precedes him? You don't know him.' She swung towards her mother. 'A moment ago you said he's a stranger to you. Well, he deserves to be known better and I will not confess to compromising my virtue by exchanging conversation with him. My conscience is clear that I have done nothing wrong. Nothing.'

Her father said, 'You have done everything wrong, my girl, and you are never to see this man again. Do you know where he lodges at this moment?'

Why did her father want to know where David was? To confront him, warn him off? She shrank at the idea and decided to give her father old news. 'At the New Liffey hotel.'

'Right,' Thomas said. 'When Henry comes home, he and I will go up there and give this character a stern warning.' He turned to his wife again. 'I won't have a common seaman near my daughter.'

'He's a carpenter-mechanic, Father, and an educated one.'

Thomas swung back at her. 'I wouldn't care if he was fit to be master of Noah or an Oxford scholar, Jane. He is no longer in your life. Do you understand me?'

Jane looked at him, hoping she could keep David's work at Mosman Cove a secret from her family. David had weeks more in Sydney—they'd have to find another way to meet. 'I understand, Father.'

At nine o'clock that same night, Henry and Thomas Wilson were making their way up Charlotte Place towards the New Liffey hotel.

Henry said to his father, 'I'm sorry I didn't tell you about that fellow when he whisked Jane away from the water, but I never dreamed he'd go after her and try meeting her in private! I think it must be him; she said he was an American whaler.' He slowed down to let his father catch up, and said, 'I can sort of understand why she'd be partial to him, though. Not bad looking, and speaks well, apart from the accent, of course.'

Thomas was panting from the walk. 'All that's immaterial, Henry! He's far from a gentleman and he's acted since like a devious rogue. Everything I hear about these Yankees marks them as a common breed. Education and money, even if his parents had both, would be lost on a man like him: money can't buy you breeding.'

'Well, he has at least the *manners* of a gentleman. And he's not just a common seaman: he has a trade.' Henry laughed. 'Like me, I suppose.'

'What? He's *nothing* like you, my son. He belongs on the high seas, and thank God he'll be out of Sydney soon. Those ships never stay here long. He'll be gone before we know it, and I'll give him a flea in his ear to send him off. Here we are, and I'll do the talking.'

The two men walked into the New Liffey and picked their way through the crowd of patrons. Thomas Wilson approached the bar. 'Is the licensee in?'

The barman looked up from pulling beer. 'Mrs Sampson is in the cellar. She won't be long.'

'I don't want to see a woman,' Thomas said. 'I want to see the man who runs this place.'

The barman stood straight and looked him in the eye. 'Mrs Judith Sampson is the licensee of this hotel. Do you want to meet her or not?'

Thomas shook his head. 'What is this world coming to? Women running things, by God. All right, all right. Tell her when she comes out that Thomas Wilson and his son want to see her.' He turned away without waiting for a reply, and he and Henry took a table within view of the bar.

Five minutes later, an attractive woman in her thirties approached the table. She nodded to both men and sat down with a pleasant, confident look. 'I'm the licensee. How can I help you?'

'You have a lodger here by the name of Milligan?'

Judith Sampson seemed to consider Thomas Wilson. She knew who he was, probably, as a grain supplier, but she had never bought from him; they'd dealt with someone else for years. She didn't seem to like his abruptness or his tone. 'And why would you want to know that?'

'Do you, or don't you?' Thomas Wilson was irritated. He didn't want questions from this woman, just answers.

When Mrs Sampson sat back, annoyed, Henry intervened, even though his father had asked him not to. 'We are not the law, Mrs Sampson, and we're not bailiffs wanting money from the man. We would just like to talk to him. There is a person in Sydney who's met him previously but doesn't know where he lives, and he wants us to pass on a message.'

Judith looked at the son. 'There is a David Milligan who keeps a room with us, but he's not here during the working week and we hardly see him. So I'm sorry to say he's not here tonight. And I can't tell you when next he'll turn up. May I pass on anything to him from you, when next I see him?'

Thomas said, 'When is he here most often? Saturdays, Sundays?'

'The latter,' Judith Sampson said in a calm voice. 'Do you live locally?'

'Near enough, ma'am,' Henry said, rising to his feet and giving his father a significant look. It was pointless hanging around this uncooperative woman's noisy bar. To his relief, his father rose, too. 'Thank you and good night.'

* * *

Four days later, on a hot Saturday night, David Milligan was playing cards at the New Liffey. Going to the bar to buy another round of drinks, he thought about what Judith Sampson had told him. A middle-aged man and his son were enquiring after him, and to his dismay their names were Thomas and Henry Wilson. It wasn't good.

'Four ales, please,' David said to the barman and waited for the beers. He had broken social conventions by meeting and corresponding with Jane, which to any protective father was a sin. But he had not harmed her and he hadn't meant to damage her reputation. He loved her, for God's sake, and he wanted to marry her. He felt a new resolve. If the chance came, he wouldn't resile from meeting the Wilsons, father and son. In fact, maybe he could convince them of his character and intentions. 'Thank you,' he said to the barman. He placed his beers on a tray and took them back to the table.

When David placed the tray on the gambling table, he saw that Jack Prendergast was seated opposite his own chair. Not a welcome face.

Prendergast leered at David. 'Not here to pick a fight, friend. Just here for a jar and a few rounds.'

David nodded and took up the cards dealt to him. For the first three hands, his luck wasn't good and Prendergast's spirits rose in consequence.

'Knew I could beat you,' Prendergast said. 'Just took a bit of time.'

David ignored him, as did the other players, and they continued the game. David drank another beer, brought to him by the next person to shout, and played three more hands, all of which he won. Prendergast's earlier good spirits evaporated.

'You're doing it again, Milligan,' he said. 'You're cheating.'

'Give it a break, will you, Jack?' the man next to him said. 'It's just a game and you're only down a few coins.'

Prendergast threw down his cards in disgust. 'It's not the losses, it's the cheating I can't abide. And I won't.' He stood up, leaned across the table and grabbed David's lapels, drawing him upwards. 'You need to be taught a lesson, cheat.' Prendergast drew back his left fist and swung. David was prepared for this, blocked it with his right and threw a straight left, which caught Prendergast flush on the jaw. Prendergast went down and David rubbed his knuckles, ready for the next phase of the fight. He wasn't walking away from this one. Prendergast got up, pushed his chair away and faced David.

'Righto!' Once again, Michael Sampson had come up behind David without anyone noticing. All eyes at the table now turned to Sampson as he said, 'You're out of here, Jack. And don't come back. You're gone from these premises for good—you hear me?'

Prendergast's chest heaved as he wiped blood from his mouth. 'He's a cheat, Sampson, I tell you.'

Sampson looked at the other players. 'Any of you say the same thing?' Two of them looked down and the third one shook his head. 'I didn't think so. You're gone, Jack, on your horse. Now.'

Prendergast didn't move, so Sampson made a move towards him. At that, Prendergast threw his arms up. 'I am going. I won't stay in this pub that robs men of their wages.' He looked at Milligan with venom in his stare. 'You'll keep, sailor. You'll keep.' He shoved his chair out of the way, then left the hotel.

The crowd started talking again around them as if this was a common event, which of course it was, but David said, 'If you fellas don't mind, I'll call it a night.'

'All right by me, Milligan,' one player said and his two mates nodded. David took his remaining drink and takings and was walking past the bar when a man put himself in his way. David recognised him at once: it was Jane's brother, Henry. He did not look hostile, but on the other hand he didn't look friendly, either.

'Mr Milligan,' Henry said. 'My father and I were here during the week looking for you.'

David felt a little irritated by the whole evening, and this man wasn't improving it. 'Well, you've found me. What can I do for you?'

Henry looked at him for some time. 'Do you mind sitting at the bar with me for a moment? Let me buy you a drink.'

Resigned to talking to one of Jane's family, which was after all what he'd been thinking about all week, David sat down at the end of the bar and gestured to the stool beside him. 'Up to you but I can do without the drink, thank you.'

When Henry sat down, the barman came up to them, but Henry gave him a quick shake of the head. After the barman had moved away, Henry turned to David and said straight out, 'You have been meeting my sister behind our backs.'

It couldn't be denied. 'We have been meeting, yes. But all our exchanges have been innocent. I respect your sister.'

Henry nodded. 'That's what Jane tells me, and I believe her. But you'll agree, Milligan, that on the surface you're not the sort of man my sister should get serious about. You're an American, you're a whaler, and you won't be in Sydney for long. Yet for some reason she is attracted to you, and for her sake we need to find out a little more about you. I came here tonight with my father's permission. What are you up to with my sister?'

David said, 'Nothing dishonourable.' Henry raised an eyebrow at this and David went on, 'We sailors have a poor reputation, Mr Wilson, I know that. Yet we are not all amoral and there are some good ones amongst us. No, I'm not perfect, but my approaches to your sister have been straightforward and respectful.' He glanced at a well-developed, cheaply dressed woman in the corner who was laughing with another man and flirting with him. The man was a sailor. Henry Wilson followed his gaze and David said, 'If I wanted that sort of female companionship, Mr Wilson, that's what I'd be doing, too. But I think of your sister and my love is sincere. My intentions are honourable: I cannot think of anything more wonderful than marrying her one day.'

Henry Wilson looked surprised, then disbelieving. 'That's all talk, sir, in your circumstances!' He went on in a less forceful tone, 'Your ship must be due to leave Sydney soon. So you'll be gone … when?'

David decided not to mention the Mosman Bay project, since Henry Wilson seemed unaware of it. 'We'll be gone once the *Cyprus* has her new mizzen mast.'

Henry nodded. 'You know of course that my father has forbidden Jane to see you.'

'I know,' David said, 'but would he see any harm in my meeting *you* again over the next two weeks? I appreciate your talking to me tonight. I'd like more time. I'd like to convince you that my intentions towards your sister are entirely honourable.'

David could see that he had taken Jane's brother aback by this suggestion.

In response, Henry Wilson stood up and put on his hat. 'Let me think about that, Mr Milligan. Let me think on that.' He turned and left the bar.

* * *

David Milligan was at St Philip's Church the next day, Sunday 1 February. He was in the back row, while the Wilson family were in the second front row, having arrived before him. He was in two minds about what he would do when the service finished. Could he pay his respects to them? After the conversation the previous night, Henry was unlikely to snub him on the spot. But the parents might be unimpressed by a direct approach. He tried to concentrate on the minister's sermon, which happened to be based on the sixth commandment: Thou shalt not kill. Very apt, considering the lawlessness of The Rocks and Sydney town.

At the end of the service, David remained seated and watched as the Wilson family got to their feet. His eyes went at once to Jane's slender form, but it was suddenly caught by her father's. He had had a good look at the man from behind, of course, on the first Sunday when he trailed him down through The Rocks to George Street, but that had been in bright sunlight. This morning, in the dimness of St Philip's, David was struck by the idea that he had seen him more recently. His shortness and the set of his head over his sloping shoulders seemed disturbingly familiar.

David stood up just as the family came up the aisle. He managed not to exchange a glance with Jane, in case that alarmed her parents. But he found his gaze flicking to the father, and for the first time got a really good look at his face. David froze in shocked recognition: this was the man who had fought with and killed Peter Ryan!

David was staring at a killer, without a doubt. And Wilson knew it: as he passed David their gazes locked and David could tell the man was recalling the searing moment of the lightning strike, when they could see each other's figures outlined with brutal clarity. It was over in a fraction of a second: Wilson's eyelids flickered and then he looked straight ahead.

As Jane passed David, she gave him a look of curiosity and concern. No wonder, David thought: his own expression was one of shock. He hung back between the pews, trying to collect himself. God, the killer of Peter Ryan was Jane's father! David was as sure of that as knowing the difference between a sperm whale and a blue whale.

For ten o'clock in the morning in summer, the air temperature in the church was mild, but David was perspiring. He'd worked his way through one dilemma: whether or not to tell the police what he'd witnessed that night in Sussex Street. Now he was faced with a worse problem, because he had just seen the culprit walk past him—Jane's father! For a moment he felt paralysed. Then on a brave impulse he walked out of the church.

Jane was outside. She and her family were about to move away but she glanced around at him. She smiled at him, and her expression turned to surprise when he walked straight up to them.

'Good morning to you all,' David said. He bowed his head to Jane, then Henry. 'Miss Wilson. Mr Wilson.' Then he looked at both parents. 'I'm David Milligan.'

Jane gazed at him without speaking. David thought he saw a glint of a smile on Henry's face. Mrs Wilson's face registered shock and

Wilson senior was so disconcerted that his expression froze and he took a step back.

David said to him, 'I know it's not the done thing to approach you like this, but we do attend the same place of worship. I'd like you to speak with me man to man about my relationship with your daughter. Either now or at some other time.'

Thomas Wilson looked around to check that no other parishioners were near enough to hear the exchange, then stepped forward, gripped David's elbow and turned him away from his family.

Wilson hissed at David, 'Your behaviour is disgraceful. You have no right to even mention my daughter to me. Good day, sir.'

'Hear him out, father,' Jane said behind them, 'or I'll make a scene.' Thomas Wilson glared at her but Jane's face remained defiant. 'I will.'

'Jane!' Anne Wilson exclaimed.

Wilson let go of David and took a deep breath. David could tell the man was feeling overwhelmed, and Jane would not be the only concern on his mind: he now knew David was a witness to Ryan's death. Wilson struggled with himself, then said shortly, 'You have two minutes, sir, and no more.'

David took his cue with relief and hope. 'I know I've gone the wrong way about recommending myself to your daughter, and I want to make amends. I'm requesting the right to call on your daughter again, but at times and places that you approve.'

'Is that all, young man?' Wilson said with sarcasm. However, looking into those angry eyes, David thought he could see fear lurking as well.

David was not going to let Wilson drive him away from Jane. 'Sir, I am an honest man with good intentions. If I might speak with your daughter in the company of—'

'I forbid anything of the sort,' Wilson said, 'and this conversation is at an end.' He paused as though weighing up his options. David sensed that uncertainty about his own safety prevailed over anxiety for his daughter. 'I will grant you this, however. If you must persist in approaching me, I give you leave to come to my office on Tuesday evening, at six.' He pulled out a card and gave it to David. 'Goodbye, young man. Come, everyone.' Wilson turned away and his obedient family followed him down the street.

David watched Jane leave, knowing she would not provoke her father by turning around to wave to him, but wishing she could. He hardly knew what to make of the complex situation he was in with regard to her father. But some decisions were required, if he and Jane were to have a future together.

* * *

As the Wilsons walked to their house after the Sunday service, Thomas's thoughts were consumed by Milligan, the young man he'd seen illuminated by a bolt of lightning on that rainy Monday night in Sussex Street. What did Milligan really want? He reached home without a single clear answer in his mind, and sat down in the parlour with his chin in his hands.

'Cup of tea before lunch, Thomas?' his wife said to him. 'Thomas?'

'I'm sorry dear,' he said. 'I was thinking about church this morning, and the sermon. Yes, I would like a cup, thank you.'

His wife went to organise the tea with the cook. His son Henry sat on the lounge opposite and started reading the newspaper. Jane had gone to her room.

Henry looked up at his father. 'That David Milligan, Father: I know he's done the wrong thing by Jane, but overall, he strikes me as straight.'

Thomas became angry. 'When I asked you to see him, Henry, it was with the express instruction to keep him away from Jane. But you failed. He's dared to confront me before everyone!'

Henry shrugged. Their teas arrived, and Anne poured for both men. 'Henry,' she said firmly, 'Jane is not to see him ever again, and that's final.'

Henry picked up his teacup. 'It's your decision of course, Mother. It's just that I don't believe he's the ogre you think he is. I mean, look at him today. Presentable, polite.'

Thomas frowned at Henry. 'Son, he's a whaler with no property or prospects. I'll see him on Tuesday and make it final and clear. If he persists, I'll set the constables onto him. That will make him understand.' He ignored his tea and looked out onto George Street. Talking of constables was bravado: truth was, he wanted Milligan nowhere near them. At any time, the man could go to the police to bear witness against him for Ryan's death—and perhaps he had already tried. The idea chilled him, but he told himself that even in that extremity he could deny everything. The word of a solid trader was surely good enough against that of a feckless sailor.

Thomas Wilson decided that when he saw Milligan on Tuesday, whatever the man might say, he would tough it out. Then another thought struck him. A bad one. Perhaps Milligan wanted to blackmail him? Wanted to hold his crime over him for ever, just so the man could have Jane?

'Your tea, dear,' Anne said with a quizzical look.

Thomas forced a smile and picked up his teacup. He made a decision: he was damned if he'd let a man like Milligan hold him at a disadvantage.

* * *

On Tuesday night, David was hurrying down York Street. He noticed that the houses along this part of York were generally grander than the dwellings in The Rocks. People of considerable wealth lived here, and to his eye their houses had moneyed gables and expensive guttering.

David was late; it was after six. Sorting problems at Mosman that afternoon had taken him longer than he liked. He hoped Wilson would still see him.

The conversation about Jane would be difficult, but the one he'd decided to have with the barley wholesaler was even more complicated. Still, David was determined to have that one first. There was no doubt in his mind that he now had to have a straight talk with

64

Wilson about Peter Ryan. He had to confirm that he was a witness to Peter Ryan's death—he didn't have the right to keep that a secret any longer.

In return, Wilson needed to be straight with David and tell him his side of the story. If Wilson was prepared to give David an honest account, it might turn out that Ryan died from striking his head when he fell; in which case Wilson was not guilty of a deliberate attempt to kill the man. David wanted to marry Jane—there had to be truth between himself and Jane's father, whatever the consequences. What David very much hoped was that he and Wilson could go together and report the incident to the police. He would be able to back Wilson up when the man explained that it was a piece of fisticuffs with an accidental outcome.

Otherwise, if David kept Wilson's secret, how could the man consider him an honest and worthy husband for his daughter? It was a risk, but for Jane's sake and his own, David had to have things out with Wilson tonight.

He went into the open yard of number 46 York Street and went to knock on the door of the office at the end, but it was open, so he entered. It was too early for lamps to be lit, and the room was dim, but it looked prosperous, like the man behind the desk.

Wilson did not rise or offer to shake hands. 'You are late, young man.'

'I'm sorry,' David said. 'Mr Wilson, before we say anything about your daughter, I'd like to discuss something else first.'

Wilson looked disconcerted, but with an effort he regained his composure. 'Sit down and get to the point.'

David took the chair opposite. 'I want to talk about the night we met in Sussex Street.'

Wilson's expression closed up. 'I don't know what you're talking about.'

'It's something I'd rather forget, but since I recognised you again on Sunday, I can't. I'll tell you what happened from my side, and I very much hope you'll tell me what happened from yours. I overheard but did not see a fight between you and Mr Peter Ryan. When it was over, I stepped out and saw you kneeling on the ground by his body. I saw your face plainly, Mr Wilson, and I'm confident that the man who got up and left the scene was you. I approached the body and found the man was dead. I didn't examine his injuries but he had no breath and no pulse.'

'Did you report this to the police?' Wilson's voice was hoarse.

'No. It wouldn't have brought the man back to life and you were gone, with no chance of my catching you up and identifying you. I could be of no help to the police, so I went back to my lodgings.'

Wilson said with a sneer, 'And kept the information to yourself.' His face hardened. 'I knew it. You want money.'

David was astonished. '*Money?* I want to have truth between us.'

'So that's the way you're putting it, you damned hypocrite! You want to blackmail me.'

David clenched his fists. 'For God's sake, how can you think that?'

'All right then, it's not for money, it's so you can keep seeing my daughter. You're offering to keep quiet about this alleged incident—with which I had nothing to do!—in return for my furthering your outrageous suit. Well, I'm not furthering anything for you, mark my words.'

Realisation brought David to his feet. 'That's a bloody insult. I came here tonight because it's your moral duty to go to the police and tell them how Peter Ryan died. As the only witness, I'm prepared to go with you and attest that it was an accident. Tell me that it was, and I'll stand by you.'

Wilson rose too, his face red with fury. 'I'm not going to the police with this, because it didn't happen. But I may go to the police and tell them I'm being blackmailed by a filthy liar and a false witness.'

David held in his own anger and said, 'You're the father of the woman I want to marry. I'm not here to condemn you—I came to know the truth, and help you if I could.'

'You're lying. Keep away from Jane and the police, young man. You're a big boy but I've taken bigger men on in the past and beaten them. If I see you with my daughter again, you'll pay dearly.' He advanced around the desk. 'Do I make myself clear?'

All at once, David felt both sickness and despair. 'Did you murder Peter Ryan?'

Wilson roared, 'I'm not answering that! Keep away from my daughter. Get out!'

David turned and left the office.

Thomas Wilson, quaking on his legs, sat back down at his desk with a thump. By God, the man had come out and said the word to his face. *Murder.* And what rot he had come out with besides. As if Thomas would go to the police and explain what happened that night! The man was an idiot. Thomas had got him completely wrong; he hadn't even had the nous to see that he could try blackmail. Well, he hadn't come for that, but now that Thomas had put the idea into his head, what would he do?

Thomas tried to work it through. The bastard could still go to the police, crying murder. But it would be Milligan's word against his own. It would all come down to a sailor, a transient American sailor of no repute, calling a leading citizen and trader a criminal.

But what if there was other evidence that the police could bring back into play once Milligan made his accusation?

And how did he know Milligan would ever cease his double pursuit? What if he kept trying to see Jane? What if he turned up on the doorstep tomorrow, demanding payment in return for his silence?

That could not be allowed to happen.

* * *

On the next day, Wednesday, Colin Smith, carpenter on board the Cockle Bay whaler, was with his labourers, busy securing the last plank to close the hole in the hull's port side. The boatswain stood back and examined the work. He nodded. 'All looks pretty good. Just get that tar onto it now. Is the cauldron ready?'

'Yes, sir,' Smith said.

'Well, take two men, bring it over here and give this a good coat.'

'Aye, aye, sir,' Smith replied. He went with two labourers amidships. There, the four cauldrons for boiling blubber, all five feet in diameter, lay idle, but a smaller one beside them was lively. The fire under it had been put out half an hour previously, but its contents would still burn a person's skin to the bone. Colin Smith's anger had been of the same temperature as the liquid tar, ever since he had not been promoted to chief carpenter after Milligan's departure. Milligan had badmouthed him to Captain Bates, Smith was sure of that, and he had a vendetta against the man now.

'Get those gloves on,' Smith said to his offsiders. 'Be careful when you pick it up. I don't want you two to get injured.'

'Big of you, Smith,' one labourer said.

'Don't give me any of your lip, Harry,' Smith said, 'otherwise I'll make it bleed. Get cracking.'

Smith took up three brushes and walked in front of the men to clear the way. While David Milligan was at Mosman Bay, he, Colin Smith would find a way to make himself a chief carpenter before too long.

* * *

It was the Thursday night following the one on which Jack Prendergast had been booted from the hotel, and Judith was having a break from her duties. She went upstairs to the children's room and found both in bed.

She looked at their sweet faces and wished that God would grant her dearest wish; she and Michael were hoping for a third child.

Five-year-old Liam was reading a book. She went over, stroked his hair and glanced down. 'You like that one, don't you?'

'Yes, Mother. Do you like books as much as me?'

Judith smiled. 'I do. I don't get much time to read, though.'

'Mr Milligan gave me this. It's about whales.' Her son paused for a moment and looked up at her. 'Is Mr Milligan sick, Mother?'

She sat alongside him and moved a hair from his forehead. 'Why would you say that, dear?'

'When he first came here, he was happy and he would sit with me and play. He made me laugh, he is funny. But last time he was sad. I asked him what's wrong and he said … it was nothing.' Her son frowned. 'I think he's sick. You need to give him special medicine, Mother.'

Judith Sampson smiled and closed his book. 'Mr Milligan is all right, Liam. He's got a big new job that's very important, and that might be worrying him, but don't you worry about *him*. Have you said your prayers?'

'Yes, Mother.'

'And cleaned your teeth?'

'That too.'

'Very good,' Judith said. Her daughter Maeve was nearly asleep, and she kissed them both goodnight. She extinguished the lamp in their bedroom and closed the door. She had five minutes before she had to go back to the bar, and she went to her own bedroom and sat down on the bed.

From the mouths of babes, Judith thought. She herself had noticed a change in the young man ever since the previous Sunday. He had left for the church in the morning in quite a good mood but when he'd returned, he'd looked very ill and she'd asked the reason why. It was as if he had a bout of deafness, because he just stared at her. Then he apologised and said no, that he was all right—it was just the heat and a big breakfast he'd had. Judith had gone away with mixed thoughts.

No, her younger friend was troubled. She wondered whether he felt burdened by knowing important things about Peter Ryan's murder and not having told anyone but her. Or maybe the young woman he was interested in had rejected him. She wished that he could resolve his predicament. She reached for her rosary beads and said five Hail Marys, praying that David Milligan would salve his troubled conscience or heal his broken heart.

Death on the Rocks

* * *

Early on the humid summer morning of Saturday 7 February, David Milligan took the earliest ferry boat from Mosman Bay to Sydney Cove. It was a twenty-four-footer that could carry six passengers and as the four oarsmen plied the way across, David thought again about the problems he was facing. First, he knew who had caused Peter Ryan's death—or, considering Wilson's savage reaction, probably murder—and he hadn't told anybody but Judith Sampson. The second was that the murderer now recognised him as the only witness to the crime. The third was that he had still to win the heart and hand of Jane Wilson—and that was now next to impossible. What a disaster. During the thirty-five-minute trip he came up with not one solution to these three problems.

Nonetheless, after landing at the Government Wharf, he set off for George Street and Jane's house. Behind him, the harbour shimmered in the sunshine, its blueness reflecting the cobalt sky. On the Sunday night previous, he'd left another note for Jane under the garden toolbox. In it he'd made no mention of the horrible moment when he recognised her father on the Sunday morning, or of the inconclusive conversation he'd had with him on the Tuesday night. Soon he was at the back fence and the gate. There was no one beyond in the garden. He reached underneath to the timber toolbox and withdrew a leather satchel, the repository for their letters. He opened it and to his delight found a new note from her. He wanted to read it then and there, but that would not be wise. Into the satchel he put his own note, which he'd written the previous night. It contained nothing that a young lady could object to: just more of his own personal history.

He put the satchel in their hiding place and set off for the New Liffey.

* * *

During the next week, Thomas Wilson was busy consolidating his orders to the barley retailers who were supplying a dozen hotels in Sydney. It was a task he usually enjoyed: haggling over contracts and getting the best deal for himself. In most instances he got what he wanted. But his otherwise successful week was clouded by his obsession with David Milligan. His contacts at the waterfront had informed him that Milligan's whaling ship, *Cyprus*, was now scheduled to be moored in Port Jackson for six more weeks. That wasn't good news for him. Time was not on his side.

Two things would happen now, he was sure. One, Jane would try to see Milligan somehow, and that would only strengthen her feelings for the man and draw her closer to him. There was no use trying to talk her out of the liaison with such a low character: love had already made her blind. He could not lock her in her room—well, he could, but that tactic was impractical and cruel. The other, much more worrying matter, was that Milligan would go to the police, or make another attempt at blackmail—threatening to make Wilson's story public. Blast the man.

That night in bed, as Anne lay sleeping beside him, Thomas had a strange thought. Just when Milligan was trying to throw his guilt in his face, he realised his conscience was now clear over Peter Ryan. The man had died by accident. The fight had been fair, but misadventure had intervened and that was that. He wouldn't let that man's death haunt him any longer.

Meanwhile Milligan was making a nuisance of himself. Was there some way of getting rid of him, keeping him permanently quiet? Another accident? Drastic and dangerous, but the death of a common sailor would scarcely throw the people and the police of The Rocks into turmoil. Milligan was after all just a Yankee seaman; there would be less hue and cry than if the victim was one of their own. And there was another reason for putting paid to Milligan: it would banish him from Jane's life. It was vital to Thomas Wilson to maintain his standing in society and his influence in business. Nothing must thwart his plans for his family, or his enterprises. Nothing.

Chapter Four

David Milligan was looking forward to meeting Jane. In her last note to him she had told him she would be at the fête in the grounds of St Philips Church on Saturday afternoon, St Valentine's Day, which was today. She would be managing a stall there with her mother, selling cakes to raise money for the church. If Mr Milligan was available, she would find an excuse to slip away and meet him. David was excited: her last note to him contained endearments which had crossed the threshold from friendship to something more serious. She had written in that vein, she said, because they could not talk face to face. *My dear one, when we do, I want you to know my true feelings for you.* He had written back the previous Sunday night, trying to tell her about his own feelings.

On St Valentine's Day he got the ferry across Port Jackson and arrived at the New Liffey feeling good.

'Whatever you're doing in Mosman Bay must be a tonic for you, David,' Judith Sampson said. 'You seem in good fettle.'

'I am indeed, thank you,' he said, 'and I'm looking forward to some of your good cooking and hospitality.' He paused. 'Tell me, as a woman of the world …' She laughed but he went on, 'What would be a good present for a young woman who has yet to fall completely for my charms and be in love with me?'

'A present? Well, things have moved on in your life, I see.'

'Perhaps. Not as much as you think and not as much as I want. But I would like to give her some sign of my affection, put it that way.'

'I think a handkerchief would be most suitable. There's a shop in York Street that sells them. I'll write down the address.' She did so. 'Here you are,' she said, giving him a slip of paper. 'Good luck! Now, I must be about my duties. Will I see you tonight?'

'You will, Judith. Goodbye.'

David went up to his room, which smelled musty after his absence. A shelf by his bedside still held three books that Judith had loaned him, and he made a mental note to return them. On his bed was a note, which he unsealed and read at once.

It was very short, and signed only 'TW', but he had no trouble guessing who the initials stood for. The man wanted to meet him tonight, at nine o'clock, at the Triumph hotel in Fort Street. He gave no reason for the summons, and David could not decide whether to feel hope or foreboding. Wilson might have second thoughts about his guilt and want to do something about it—or he might not. David put the note with Jane's letters, which were tucked into his journal.

By mid-afternoon, David had purchased his present to Jane and had it gift wrapped. It was safely in his pocket as he made his way to the fête at St Philip's. There were eight stalls set up and the crowd was thick, picking up fresh produce and bric-a-brac. When David approached Jane's stall he was careful not to go too close, and pulled his hat lower. He watched Jane's mother handing over a cake to a smiling buyer. Jane was at the back of the stall, preparing something. David circled the store and got her attention without her mother seeing. Jane's eyes lit up and she smiled at him. He returned the smile and his heart pumped harder. He wandered around the rest of the stalls, then spotted her heading around the back of the church, carrying a basket.

He followed, and in a deserted area behind the church they stood face to face. It was the first time that they had seen each other alone and with no fence between them. He was so overcome that words failed him.

It was Jane who spoke first. 'Thank you for coming. I really hoped you would.'

He gave her his present. 'Happy Saint Valentine's Day.'

She put her basket down and opened the little package. 'How nice! It's very pretty. Thank you.' With a pleased smile, she slipped it into a pocket with the scrap of paper and the ribbon.

He took her hands, which she didn't refuse.

She murmured, 'I can't stay long. I just told my mother I needed to get more jam from the store. Let's go in, there's no one about.' She picked up the basket, beckoned him with her other hand and led him into a little outbuilding at the back of the church, which was dim and deserted. She took three jars of jam from a shelf and lowered them into her basket. As she stood up, he bought her close and kissed her on the cheek.

She drew back a little and touched her face where he'd kissed her. 'Mr Milligan.'

'I'm sorry, Miss Wilson. Just had to do that.'

She came closer again, not touching him, just looking into his eyes. 'I have missed you this week. All I wanted was to be with you. There, I've said it. I am brazen.'

'You are not. You could never be that.' He paused, then said, 'Is your father still telling you that you can't see me?'

She closed her eyes. 'Yes.'

She said no more, and he wondered whether she knew that Wilson had demanded to see him. Probably not, and he couldn't bear to ask her. He had a strong sense that the meeting at the Triumph hotel was not going to be in his own favour. He felt a surge of rebellion. 'Is there any way you could snatch an hour or two with me some time?'

She opened her eyes and beamed at him. 'I've thought of that, and yes I can. It's going to be risky, but I don't care. I need to see you for longer than a few minutes.'

'So do I! Only seeing you once a week is torture.'

'My parents and Henry will be out of the house next Wednesday night, for three hours. They have a function to attend. Mother has instructed my friend Mary to stay with me. I know she's done that because she wants someone to watch over me.' Jane smiled. 'But Mary is a dear friend and she declines to be a watchdog! I've confided in her about you and she won't say anything if you visit me. Please come to the gate at seven-thirty in the evening. Can you?'

'*Can I?* This is wonderful!'

Through the open door of the storeroom, they could hear footsteps approaching down the side of the church. Jane quickly pulled David out into the sunlight, and when one of the parishioners walked by, they were more than a yard apart and Jane was rearranging the jars of jam in her basket. When they were alone again she whispered, 'I have to go. It's best if I walk back on my own. I'm sorry … David.'

He was thrilled at hearing his given name for the first time. 'Wednesday night then … Jane.'

She smiled wickedly and went off.

* * *

At eight-forty-five that night, David made his way from Cumberland Street onto Princes Street, then down along Fort Street. It was far from a fine street; it was strewn with debris and many of the buildings were poorly constructed. Gangs of boys clustered at corners, and women in pairs chatted at open doorways; at this time of an evening, it was one of the noisiest places in Sydney Cove.

David was in a better frame of mind since he had met Jane behind the church. He would be seeing her for sure on Wednesday night, having worked out how to get away from Mosman Bay; he had a meeting with a timber supplier in town that afternoon, so could see Jane later. He was also hopeful about the meeting with Thomas Wilson. There was still a chance to convince him to go to the police, with himself as a supporting witness. If the police were sceptical about his coming forward so late in the day, David could tell them the truth—that he had only recognised Thomas Wilson recently. Wilson would be held to account for what he'd done to Ryan, but the charges might not be as serious as the man obviously feared, and he was not a hardened criminal but a respected citizen. He would be charged with assault, but when the police established all the facts, perhaps he would be spared a charge of manslaughter? David had no idea: he did not know the colony's laws.

When David walked into the public bar of the Triumph, he found it a low dive compared with the New Liffey. It was mean and small and its patrons suited the surroundings; in fact Jack Prendergast was there, gambling with friends. There were loose-looking girls present, including a bright-haired woman at the bar. David spied Thomas Wilson at a side table, giving him a wave. David went and joined the man, who offered no handshake, though there was a beer waiting for David on the tabletop.

'Sit down,' Wilson said, and paused, looking hard at David as he did so. Eventually Wilson said, 'My son Henry seems to have a notion that you may not be the reprobate that we thought you.'

'I'm sorry you and your wife have had a low opinion of me. But I'll be glad if you consent to know me better.'

Wilson pointed a finger at him. 'Boy, my wife and I have been protecting our daughter, that's all. And we still are. But if I'm satisfied with what you have to say to me tonight, I'm prepared to speak with my wife and smooth the troubled waters, as they say.' He grinned. 'Smooth the waters, so that you may see my daughter in our company.'

David sat back amazed, his beer untouched. 'Why the sudden change?'

Wilson laughed. 'It's simple. You can see Jane, but only if you desist with this stupid idea that I had anything to do with the death of Peter Ryan. That is sheer fantasy on your part, Milligan. If you want to see my daughter, you will put aside fantasies. Do I make myself clear?'

David's ears pricked up. Wilson was not plainly denying that he had confronted Ryan on Sussex Street that rainy Monday night! Which meant he was not denying the fight; just the outcome. It was a step towards the truth and David followed it up. 'As I said to you last time, Mr Wilson, I want to help you clear up this matter. I don't believe you intended to murder Ryan.' Wilson's eyes gleamed as David went on, 'You had no hankering to kill him; you got angry and lashed out. It was an accident. I will tell that to the police when you and I see them together. Your family has a good name. If you front up to the police with honesty and my support, and accept whatever charges they may bring, your reputation may suffer for a while, but it will be restored because of your courage.'

In answer, Wilson cursed and banged his fist on the table, which upset his own beer, and brought glances from the adjoining patrons, including the woman at the bar, who now had a bottle of gin in front of her. Wilson leaned forward. 'Understand this, boy. I will not go to the police, and nor will you. Here's my instruction: it's so simple, even a dimwit like you can understand it. If you want to see my daughter Jane, you'll drop this subject and stay silent on it for ever.'

David sat back, appalled. He was getting nowhere with this man, who had now stooped to bargaining with his own daughter's virtue to keep his own secrets!

'You are thinking about it, aren't you?' Wilson said with a leer.

David had to swallow his disgust to continue talking to the man. 'The more you say about the subject of Ryan's death, Mr Wilson, and the more you forbid me to mention it, the more guilty you sound. Regardless of how I feel about your daughter, I can no longer avoid going to the police. I suggest you accompany me, but whether you do or not, I will tell them that you were there that night, and offer myself as a witness to Ryan's death.'

'I wouldn't do that if I were you, boy.'

'That sounds like a threat, Mr Wilson. I don't like threats.'

Wilson said nothing for some time, then said more calmly than David had expected, 'Very well, do it and be damned. You're forfeiting any chance of ever seeing my daughter again, but go to the police and see if it does you any good or me any harm. It won't, I tell you. All they'll have is your description of a man seen at a distance of twenty feet in the pouring rain on a dark night. They'll have the testimony of a rat-arsed foreign sailor against a prominent citizen of this colony. They'll throw you out the door.'

David got to his feet, almost bumping into the bright haired woman from the bar, who was passing the table and heading for the street. 'I love Jane, sir, and you're her father. But if I didn't do this, I'd have no respect for myself. And nor would she.'

Wilson's eyes flashed and his body tensed, almost as though he were about to throw himself across the table at David. But he did not move, he just said in a low voice, 'Good night.'

David turned and walked out onto the street, his mind in turmoil at what he had just done. He had put yet another bar between himself and Jane. He was about to betray her own father to the law! It had been bad enough struggling for ways to see her, to work for their future together, to deserve her ... but she had loved him throughout. Now she would hate him, for bringing her father into disgrace. His heart ached and his steps slowed. He came to a stop in the dark, between two street lamps. Could he go back and plead with the man again?

He was alone. The noisy lads were gone and all the front doors down the length of the dirty street were closed. He turned to the wall beside him, put his hands against the rough stone, still warm from the day's heat, and hung his head, trying to find the best solution to this dilemma—the best for Jane, for himself.

He was so lost in despair that he did not hear the footsteps behind him until it was too late. He still had his arms up, he was defenceless, when he turned at the hurried sound and saw the twisted, angry face of Thomas Wilson.

A searing pain went through his abdomen, his arms dropped and the terrible face vanished. Dizziness overcame David and he slipped to the ground, his gaze sliding down the wall until he was level with the pavement. That shadowy sandstone surface was the last thing he saw before his eyes closed.

Thomas Wilson stared down at the bloodied knife in his hand. Seconds passed, then he shook himself and looked around. There was a thud in the darkness nearby; whether an animal or a human had moved, he did not know. Before the creature came into sight, he had to get rid of the weapon and then walk down the street as though he'd done nothing, seen nothing.

He stepped around Milligan's lifeless body, forced himself to walk casually forward, and dropped the knife into a pile of debris that lay a few yards on, in someone's dark front yard. He could hear no steps behind him; he must have been mistaken and the noise had not been on the street but inside a house. It would have been safer to dispose of it more securely, somewhere else, but he had panicked. Too late to worry about that. More important to get himself well clear.

Wilson marched down Fort Street and all the way to Argyle Street without seeing anyone behind him or before. It was not until he turned into George Street that the shock of the crime gripped him. Sweat enveloped him and he started to shiver. He had killed once before, yes. He had killed Peter Ryan, by accident. But this was murder. Tonight he'd taken a sheath knife to the meeting with Milligan, worn at the waist under his coat. He'd told himself he'd only use it to threaten Milligan. But he'd used it for murder.

* * *

Lizzie Robinson, having downed her beer at the bar in the Triumph, had decided to invest in a bottle of gin, and when it was time to leave she'd decided to take it home before she went on to do her night's work. Her place was just along the street from the pub, a front room in a decrepit lean-to between two more solid houses. Putting her bottle on the table by her window, she'd heard footsteps outside and peered through the gap in her curtains—you never knew when a likely customer would come by.

It was the good-looking, fair-haired man she'd nearly bumped into in the bar. His face looked grim; not a likely customer, more's the pity. She was just regretting that when she heard more footsteps and bent across the table to look out again, only to see the man's companion from the bar walk up the street. He looked grim, too—was he after the younger one? If so, maybe she could scream out and warn him?

She went out onto her three foot wide verandah and peered down the street. It was just as she'd feared, but ten times worse, and she had no time to scream or do anything to prevent it, because the older man was onto the younger before he even knew what was happening, and a second later he was on the ground, and the other was standing over him holding a knife. Terrified, Lizzie darted back into her room. She managed to close her front door quietly so as not to alert the killer, but when she went towards the window to pull the curtains closer, she knocked the bottle of gin to the floor and it landed with a thump that sounded to her like a clap of thunder. She bent down and checked that it hadn't broken, and then a horrible fascination gripped her and she leaned over to peer through the gap in the curtain again. Only to see the killer walk away down her street, fling the knife aside before he'd gone more than a few yards, and disappear out of view.

Was the young man dead, or wounded and in need of help? It took all her courage to open her door and step onto the verandah again, but she had to find out. She looked along the street first, to be sure that the killer was out of sight, then ran to the man on the ground. He was lying on his stomach and his blond hair was askew. She pushed with all her strength to turn him over. Yes, he was the young man from the Triumph bar, and he was still breathing, though blood covered his chest and stomach, and was pooling under him. His eyes were closed but his mouth opened and she leaned closer and laid her hand over his heart, trying to feel the beat.

'Wilson,' the victim said, 'Jane Wilson.' He closed his eyes and the chest on which Lizzie's hand was resting expelled one more breath, then was still. The young man was dead.

She was witness to murder, and she knew where the weapon was, too. She ran along the street, bent over the pile of debris and quickly found the knife. Holding it by its tip, she grabbed a discarded piece of newspaper and wrapped the knife in it. What to do now? What could a person like her do with this evidence? Appalled by the crime, but finding no solutions, all she could do was walk the short distance to the brothel where she worked, and put off any decisions until the morning.

The young man's face came back to her, not just from the pub but from before the new year. He'd come into Madame Greta's place with some friends. She would have given him a roll for free because he was so cute, but although he'd been laughing and jolly then, he'd not chosen any of the girls, let alone her. He might have been a cherry, she thought, or queer, but in the end she decided he was a true man, and a nice one. And now he was dead.

Hiding the paper-covered knife under her shawl, Lizzie pushed open the brothel door and nodded to the sixteen-stone man keeping guard. Going down the corridor, she thought about the murderer, who'd been sitting in the Triumph talking to the man he was going to kill, as though it was just a normal night. Thomas Wilson was known to her and to everyone in this house. He was a regular, who'd come even more often this year, usually during the week, and none of the girls liked him because he could be rough. Madam permitted this because he paid well, but Lizzie didn't care how much he paid; she made sure she kept well clear of him. As a twenty-six-year-old she was past her prime and he'd never picked her. She'd felt relief at this, and pity for the younger women who had to put up with him.

'You took your time, Lizzie,' the ageing matron said. 'Fix yourself up in your room, there's a good love, then come straight down. It's a big night.'

Lizzie did as she was told. She washed and changed in her room, and hid the knife. Then wondered why she'd kept it. Keep quiet would be the best way! If she grassed on Wilson, he would get off scot-free because he was a toff and she a street girl, and after that she'd be fair game to him, she'd be in danger every minute. Wilson could take care of her like she was a bag of unwanted kittens dumped from the wharf in Sydney Cove. No, quiet she'd keep.

* * *

Judith Sampson was in the New Liffey hotel at eight o'clock on the following morning. On most Sunday mornings, when she had a break from her children, she would take time off and say her prayers. There was no church for her to attend and, like most Catholics in The Rocks, the Sampsons were not pious or churchgoing. She was near to the end of her chores when she heard the front door ring. She opened it and was greeted by two constables. She didn't know them, and they weren't the ones who had been enquiring before, about Peter Ryan's death.

'Good morning, ma'am. Could we talk to you?'

Judith opened the door wider and gestured them in. She led them to a tidy corner table. 'How can I help you?'

The constable extracted something from his jacket pocket and showed it to her. It was a key, with a tag labelled 'New Liffey Hotel'.

'Can you confirm that this is one of your keys, ma'am?'

Judith nodded. 'Yes, it is. Where did you find it?'

'On the body of a young man,' the constable said.

'You mean a dead body?' Judith felt a sense of dread coming on. She sat down on the chair opposite them, trying to prepare herself for the answer.

'Yes.' The constable brought out a notebook. 'About six feet, early twenties, blond hair, big frame. There was a letter on him, addressed to a David Milligan.'

Judith forced her eyes shut and her ears started to ring. The constable was talking to her, but it was if she were six feet underwater.

'Ma'am? Ma'am? Did you hear me?'

Judith forced herself to concentrate. 'I'm sorry. Go on.'

'Do you know this man? Is he a lodger here?'

'Yes, he is,' Judith said, then gasped and corrected herself. 'He was. Dear God Almighty. What happened to him?'

'He died of knife wounds to the chest and stomach. Do you know of any family or connections who might identify him?'

She gripped the edge of the table, hardly able to speak. 'No, no family.' She tried to rally. 'He's a whaler, off the American ship, *Cyprus*. You could apply to the captain.'

'We'd like the corpse identified as soon as possible, ma'am. If you'd be so good, would you mind coming to the morgue?'

Judith shuddered at the awful word. *Dead*. That lively young man was no more.

'Ma'am?'

'It's a horrible thing for a person to have to do, Constable, but I will come with you. Now?'

'If you wouldn't mind, ma'am, it would help our investigation. The morgue is not far from here.'

Judith turned around to see Michael coming down the stairs. 'Dear,' she said to him as he approached, 'I have some terrible news. David Milligan has been found murdered.'

'We're not yet defining it as murder, sir,' the constable said. 'But the stab wounds on his body could not have been self-inflicted. It does appear that he met foul play.'

Michael was horrified. 'That's terrible.'

'They want me to look at the body, Michael,' Judith said feeling her strength ebb from her. 'I'll be away a little while.'

'I can do that if you want, love. Leave it to me.'

Judith shook her head. 'No, I'll go.' She walked to the door and the two constables followed her out into the street. Then she turned to them. 'You still have his key. Don't you want to look in his room?'

'Yes, but we must identify him first. Please keep his door locked until we return, Mrs Sampson, and allow no one inside. Allow us to accompany you to the morgue. This way; it's in Jamieson Street.'

Walking with the policemen and ignoring curious passers-by, Judith struggled to control her shock. And that shock was starting to be infiltrated by sadness. Tears were approaching but she forced them away. She owed it to David Milligan to find out exactly how he died. 'Constable, I've seen brawls in my hotel, and legs broken and wounds inflicted. Please don't think me queasy about the human body and what can be done to it. You don't need to spare me the details; let me hear what you think happened to Mr Milligan.'

The constable gave her a glance of respect and said, 'He had been stabbed, ma'am, that was clear. He may also have been injured in other ways; we won't know that until the surgeon's had a look at him. So, he was attacked by a person or persons unknown. Cause of the attack is also unknown, except it's unlikely to have been theft. In one pocket he still had his wages packet, with money inside it.' They walked a little further, turned right and started going downhill, past Gloucester Street. Below them, the harbour shimmered so brightly it was hard to look at.

'He wasn't the kind of man to get into a street brawl,' Judith said.

'Ma'am, he was a seaman,' the constable said. 'Sailors on shore do as they please. They get drunk. They get mean and pick fights. They start brawls and some of them die. When we come across a victim of violence in Sydney town, ten to one the dead man will be a sailor.'

'I just told you, David Milligan wasn't a typical sailor. He was spare in his drinking, cautious in his gambling, educated in his speech, and he was well-mannered and intelligent.'

'That may well be, ma'am, but sailors get into more strife than any other men.'

Judith fell silent as they approached the morgue. She was about to see the body of a handsome, young, good-humoured man, whose death was simply a matter of cold fact to the policeman at her side.

Inside the morgue, she was escorted into a back room. On a table in the middle of it was a body covered by a large sheet. Judith shrank as she entered, not because there was the smell of death in the room, but from the certainty of whom she would see. She took in a deep breath, exhaled, and went to the side of the table. The constable lifted back the upper end of the sheet and exposed the calm face of Judith's young lodger. There was no visible blood, his eyes were closed and the fair hair was brushed back from his unlined brow.

She brought a hand to her cheek, closed her eyes and turned away. 'That's him, Constable. That's David Milligan.'

'Thank you, ma'am. Please follow me. We need you to sign a form to that effect.'

Judith followed him out to the front office, and signed the paper on the counter. 'Is there anything else I can help you with?'

'Just the search of his hotel room. We'd like you to be present, to confirm which belongings are his.'

Judith nodded. 'When would you want to do that?"

'Tomorrow, seven in the morning?'

'Yes. Of course.'

'Thank you. Speaking of possessions, I want to show you what we found on him.' He went to a shelf and extracted a box, brought it over and opened it. 'There was his hotel key, of course, a couple of papers that I won't disclose to you, and these few things. Do they look familiar?'

There was a wallet, David's wages envelope, a customs declaration from when he'd landed in Sydney, and a man's handkerchief. 'Yes, that's his wallet.' She looked at it sadly. 'If only he'd drunk in my hotel last night, he'd be alive this morning. Where was he found?'

'Not far from the Triumph hotel on Fort Street.'

'So what do they say there; was he drinking in their bar before he went out into the street and got knifed? Did anyone there threaten him? Did anyone in the street see the fight, and what about the householders in the area, did anyone hear anything?'

'Ma'am, our investigation has just begun, so I'm not at liberty to disclose what leads we may have.'

Judith looked at him bitterly. 'You mean you don't have any at all.'

The constable grimaced, and pulled over a file lying open on the counter. He tapped his finger on the top sheet. 'This is the list of murders currently under investigation by our station. You have my permission to scan it. Fifteen deaths by violence have occurred in The Rocks over the last six months and eight of the victims were sailors. Half a dozen of the cases that we've classed as murder are as yet unsolved. You will see from this, ma'am, that due to factors quite beyond police control, I cannot guarantee you that we will ever be able to arrest the murderer or murderers of Mr Milligan.'

'And what if he were English, and had gold and status, would you be more interested in getting justice done?'

'Now, don't be like that, ma'am. There are not enough of us in The Rocks and we're all busy. We have a tough job, but we do our best.'

Judith was almost ready to cry at the sadness of it all. To distract herself, she read the list of murders, noting Peter Ryan's name amongst them. 'If anyone at the hotel saw Mr Milligan last night, or has any idea what happened to him, shall I report it to you?'

'Thank you, yes, at The Rocks police station, ma'am. Before you go, can you think of anyone who's been hostile to Milligan of late? Anyone who might have had a grudge against him?'

'He wasn't a quarrelsome man, Constable. But when he was playing cards in the New Liffey one night, one of the players insulted him and tried to pick a fight. His name's Jack Prendergast. He lives near the New Liffey but we've banned him for being violent.'

The constable was writing down the name. 'Thank you for your help, ma'am. You're free to go. Goodbye.'

Judith left the morgue and walked fast to escape the smell of death. She reached for a handkerchief and dabbed her eyes. She refused to break down in public but the sadness was almost overwhelming. She thought of the awful letter that the captain of the *Cyprus* would soon be mailing to David's parents in Boston, America, the horrible news coming to the ears of the young woman in Sydney whom David had wanted to marry. These people would mourn David Milligan, and so did she, in her own way. But would anyone else care very much? The police certainly didn't; they couldn't even properly make up their minds that he'd been murdered!

But Judith was in no doubt. This was not a theft gone wrong, nor was it the result of a random brawl—it was a silent, fatal stabbing in the dark. Someone had wanted to kill David Milligan, and Judith Sampson would find out who.

Back at the pub, she felt some relief in confiding in Michael. 'I must keep busy,' she concluded. 'I'll think on it as I work.'

'You do what you must, love,' he replied.

Judith threw herself into her weekend housekeeping, which was mostly devoted to their own living quarters. She was dusting the mantel over her fireplace when she remembered the books she'd loaned David. He wouldn't need them now.

She took the spare room key from her pocket and unlocked his room, bracing herself to see it empty and forlorn. She stepped inside and looked around. He had left it neat, with the bed made and a few personal items tidy on his bedside table. She opened the window to let in some fresh air. The room looked clean enough not to shame her when the constables came on the morrow, but she inspected it anyway, looking for any clues as to where David might have been headed when he left the New Liffey and went to his death.

The wardrobe held two shirts, two pair of trousers and David's kit bag. She didn't look inside the kit bag—she should leave that to the police. She found that he only had one pair of shoes at the bottom of the wardrobe, so he must have been wearing his working boots when he died. His drawers contained undergarments and nothing else. So little in witness to the life he had led!

She sighed and went to the books in his bedside table. These were the three she'd lent him: *Ivanhoe, The Swiss Family Robinson* and *Rob Roy*. Picking them up, she found a slimmer volume beneath. It was bound in soft leather, with a clasp, and looked like a journal. Of all the items in the room, only this one promised any clues about David Milligan's recent movements. Judith could not help dropping her books on his bed and opening the clasp.

She saw at once that this was indeed his journal. As she flicked through the pages to see what he might have written in the previous days, something fell out from behind the back cover, onto the floor. Feeling like a spy, Judith bent down and picked up the letter and replaced it in the back of the journal, only to find there were other folded letters there as well. She put the book down on the table top.

She stood there, hesitating. She would invade his privacy if she read his journal. But the police would do that anyway, if they came across it next day: and were they the best people to find clues in its pages? Then there was David's secret love to consider. Anyone reading this would be privy to details about another young person's private life; her name, her family, her dealings with David … Would he have wanted her betrayed like this to unsympathetic eyes, laid open to gossip—maybe even to having her indiscretions read out in court?

Judith opened the book at the first page and at once a name leaped out at her: Jane. He had begun this diary on the very day when he had first seen the young woman at St Philips. There was little in it about his work; this was a record of his hopes and dreams and his innocent meetings with the girl he'd wanted very much to win. He never gave her surname, a protective impulse that Judith could only regret. She skimmed onward, trying not to read this intimate record of his feelings, looking for other names. He mentioned her parents, but didn't give their surname either, or their address. Then suddenly, on Monday 5 January, Jane was no longer the subject. Instead there was a description of a conflict that David had witnessed, with two folded documents lying between the next pages.

Judith recalled the date and the circumstances, because this was the fight David had confided in her about: the fight in which Peter Ryan had died, though he was not yet named. David had set down a description of the attacker: early forties, five feet six inches, brown hair, curly, about fifteen stone. David had seen the man because lightning had struck, scorching a nearby lamppost and illuminating the scene. Surely the police would be glad of this!

Judith opened the two papers. One was an invitation to Peter Ryan to meet someone that very night. The signatory's name was smeared by water damage, so only the first three letters were legible: 'Wil'. The other document, also stained, looked like a note from an assayer about a consignment of barley, addressed to Peter Ryan. She put both documents back into the journal.

Impatient to see what had occurred just before David's death, Judith turned the pages until she got to the month of February. In the entry for Sunday the first, she found Jane again, but in a quite different context. David had just recognised the man who had beaten Peter Ryan to the ground and killed him: and he now identified him as 'Jane's father'. Could this be the Jane with whom David had fallen in love?

The strange truth was confirmed in the entry for 7 February. David wrote that he was trying to convince Jane's father to go to the constables in his company, and tell them that Ryan's death was not deliberate—it was a tragic accident, the result of a fight. *I must hope that he proves himself an honourable man and consents to come with me to the police.*

Good God, Ryan's killer *was* Jane's father! No wonder the poor young man had been in a state of turmoil lately. Judith tried to get over her shock and concentrate on the last details that David had written. His own honour and decency came through but so, to Judith's dismay, did his naivety. How could he have thought that such a man would meekly cooperate with him and go to the constables after what he'd done? She shook her head and her sadness redoubled.

Love had blinded David Milligan and led him to hope for the impossible. It had also led him into a dilemma, because his beloved's father had not only banned David from seeing her but was also a murderer. Whatever David Milligan had planned to do about his dilemma, there was not a shred of possibility that he would ever have won Jane.

Judith extracted the loose documents from David's journal, sat down and put them on the coverlet. From them she assembled one pile, all on matching paper, that comprised Jane's letters to David. Apart from these there were the two papers found on Peter Ryan, and a note on different paper, folded twice, that she opened and read first. It was from a TW, summoning David to meet him at nine pm on Saturday 14 February at the Triumph hotel, Fort Street. Her heart beat fast. Was TW the last person to see David alive?

If David had kept the appointment with this man on the night he died, the police would find this out at once when they checked at the Triumph hotel in their investigation; the landlord there would no doubt be able to give the names of patrons to whom David had spoken in the bar. Door-knocking on Fort Street might uncover what had gone on there, later that night. So this note would be of no extra help to the police—but she put it in David's drawer anyway, for them to find.

As for Jane's letters, Judith was not going to leave them lying about for uncaring eyes to see. Not unless they gave clues as to why David had died. Judith flicked through them, her eyes burning, just in case, but hardly another name but David's was mentioned in them, there was not a word about any crimes, and Jane did not even sign her surname. The most recent letter went so far as to end, 'Your loving Jane', which brought tears to Judith's eyes. They were innocent, effusive, charming and sincere; worthy of the young man to whom they were written.

Judith stood up, holding the journal and Jane's letters to her chest. If anyone else deserved to see them, it was David's family. Perhaps one day she would obtain his parents' address from the captain of the *Cyprus*, and mail them to America. In the meantime, she had a deep conviction that the only person likely to figure out who had killed David was herself.

* * *

On Wednesday morning, four days after seeing David at the St Philips fete, Jane Wilson was sitting in the George Street parlour and looking forward to his visit that evening. David hadn't been at church last Sunday, but that had just made her expectations more tantalising. It had been difficult to keep her excitement in check, and her high spirits were on show, so much so that her mother had remarked on them. Jane had fobbed her off with an excuse, but her mother was suspicious. It was fortunate that her mother considered her friend Mary Fruin, who was a spinster of twenty-five years old, to be a suitable guard over her imprisonment on Wednesday night. Tonight.

Three whole hours she would spend with David, while Mary promised to read in another room. They would be close together, uninterrupted, and she wondered if he might go further than a kiss on the cheek. She coloured at her own thoughts, and to rescue herself from her mother's constant gaze, she picked up the *Gazette*. There was nothing much to read on the front of this government newspaper, apart from some official tenders and the latest political shenanigans. Just for interest, she turned to the weddings and engagement section. Maybe, not too long into the future, she might see her name and David's there. How wonderful that would be.

Jane was about to put down the paper when her eye caught the criminal section and an article about a murder of a young man found in Fort Street on Sunday morning last. Jane looked closer at the details and David Milligan's name leaped out at her, as if to grab her with both hands. The *Gazette* fell onto the floor. Jane stood up and went straight through the back part of the house to the garden. Her mother looked up, surprised, but did not follow.

Jane staggered into the most sheltered part of the garden, reached out her hand and sat down on the bench by the strawberry beds. *Murdered.* The word alone shot shivers through her. Her body was shaking now, and nausea washed through her stomach and chest. The article had listed the funeral, which would be at St Philips. The shocking words she had read repeated themselves over and over as the morning sun beat down on the greenery around her. She couldn't believe it. *Killed. To be buried.* She glanced around her, wanting to run to him, knowing she never could.

'Jane? Where have you gone, dear?' her mother called from inside.

Jane opened her mouth to reply and nothing came out. She took three deep breaths. 'I'm at the back, Mother. Just picking some strawberries.'

'You needn't bother with those. And don't be long; we have to go to the orphanage this morning. Pack some vegetables, if you will. A basketful.'

'Yes, Mother!' She stood up, lost her balance and nearly fell over. There was a rain barrel nearby. She drank some of the water, though they usually boiled it. It was so fresh and cool that she splashed more over her face.

She would never see him again. Tears started, and she let them flow. Shaking her head, she picked up a basket. Kneeling by the vegetable plot, she picked carrots and cabbages, her tears wetting their leaves. For these private moments, she gave herself over to her grief. If her ever practical mother asked her why her eyes were red, she would say she had made the mistake of touching the onions.

* * *

Judith Sampson was at David Milligan's funeral at St Philips, arranged by Captain Bates of the *Cyprus*. It was four days since David's death, a chilly Thursday in mid-February. There were few mourners: Captain Bates and one of his senior officers, herself and Michael, and a young woman in the pew nearest the church door. A poor attendance to mark the passing of a promising young man. His parents of course would not know of their son's death for many months, and that was a tragedy in itself.

It was strange to be standing in this Anglican church. Catholics with Judith's upbringing had an innate fear of other religions, which included their places of worship, and stern priests warned them off attending them. As a child in Dublin, she had once darted into a Church of England building on a dare, but she would never have dreamed of joining in a sacrament like this. Never. Yet she and Michael were quite even-minded about faith. Judith tended to think that it was the same God who reigned over most Christians, and that the same hell, the same heaven and the same saints beckoned all in the end. The minister, too, showed tolerance and charity about David's beliefs: the young Episcopalian had not been a parishioner but he had come to church on several Sundays, and his captain spoke highly of him. Judith looked around to see how the young woman at the back might be reacting to the service. But there was no one there.

Afterwards, the humble wagon that carried the coffin set off for the cemetery. She, Michael and the two officers from the *Cyprus* walked behind it down Charlotte Place to George Street, then along to the cemetery on the corner of Park and George. Pedestrians along the 'bullock trail' of the main street doffed their caps or stared in curiosity as their little entourage passed by. Judith found herself sending up silent prayers for David's soul as she walked.

David Milligan's body was interred with a few short prayers, and the mourners went back to the New Liffey, where Judith had set aside a table with refreshments. It felt like a pitifully modest wake for her young lodger. She said sadly to Bates, 'Did you know him before this voyage, Captain?'

'I did not, ma'am,' the captain said, his right hand holding a tankard of ale and his left a half-eaten meat pie. 'But I came to value him on the passage out, and I'm very sorry to lose him. He made an excellent job of the repairs to the *Cyprus* and lately he's been supervising construction work over at Mosman Bay, as no doubt you know. He came back here on weekends, did he?'

'He did, Captain.'

'He wasn't just an expert carpenter, he'd had a good education and he used his head. He could lead men, and they respected him.' The captain shook his head and finished the rest of his pie. 'This is good, ma'am, very good.'

'Thank you. You say your crew respected him—but was there anyone amongst them who didn't get on with him? Anyone who might have held a grudge?'

The captain sighed. 'Hard to say. On board ship, if you can understand it, everything happens at close quarters. Tempers can fray. There are always a few men ready to hold grudges, pick fights.'

'Any man in particular, lately? Someone who worked alongside David Milligan?'

The captain thought for a moment. 'Well, there's a whaler called Colin Smith who likes to make a nuisance of himself. I made Milligan Chief Carpenter over Smith, who was pushing for the rank himself, so he was pretty mutinous about it. The irony is, Smith will probably have David's job now, over at Mosman Bay, though he's not a patch on the dead lad.' The captain shook his head. 'No one else springs to mind. Smith is the only one I can think who might harbour any malice. Though he's more of a whinger than a real rebel.'

'Thank you. Would you like another drink?'

The captain smiled. 'Have you ever noticed a sailor refuse one, ma'am?'

Judith got up from the table. 'I will fetch you one.'

'You serve excellent grog, Mrs Sampson. In a few days' time I'll send a lad up from the docks to purchase some more beer and whisky from you.'

'My pleasure, Captain.'

Next day, Judith got through her chores early. She was no constable, but she would devote a portion of her day to working out what had happened around David Milligan on the night he died. She would investigate people, places and events. And she would begin in Fort Street.

She knew from the newspaper that his body had been found in the middle section of Fort Street, near a horse trough. She also knew, from the note from a 'TW' that she had found amongst his things, that he must have visited the Triumph hotel, in the same street, not long before he was killed. She walked past the Triumph, wondering whether she could walk in and pose a few questions later. But she didn't know the publican, and the moment he heard that she was a rival at the New Liffey, he'd probably baulk at discussing a crime committed in the vicinity of his hotel, and give her the cold shoulder.

So she walked on, towards the nearest horse trough, examining the stone paving at the side of the road, which kept people's feet off the dirt in the middle. There were vehicles and riders on the thoroughfare but this stretch of sidewalk was not busy. The only other person in sight was a young woman lingering by the trough. She was not looking Judith's way, so Judith did not feel too silly, progressing slowly up the street and keeping her gaze on the ground. Meanwhile she could see no clues as to where David had been struck down.

Then she suddenly came across the young woman; in fact she almost bumped into her, because the other was also staring at the ground and did not see Judith coming. Judith gasped, stopped and followed the direction of the young woman's gaze. She found herself looking at a section of pavement marred by rust-coloured stains. She knew what they were: dried blood. It had not rained since Saint Valentine's, the day he was killed.

Judith lifted her eyes, horrified. Her glance met the eyes of the young woman, which were red-rimmed and startled. Judith said awkwardly, 'Good morning.'

The girl took a step back. 'I'm sorry. Good morning to you.' Her voice quivered.

Judith said, 'No, I'm sorry—I startled you. Are you all right?'

'Yes, I am, thank you. I just had a funny turn.' Her eyes filled with tears.

Judith leapt right in. 'Forgive me, but I can see something is upsetting you. Is this the very spot? Do you know what happened here?'

The young woman said nothing for a while, then murmured, 'I must go. I'm sorry, goodbye.' She turned and walked away.

Judith went after her and put a hand on her arm. 'If you have the same reason as I to come here today, it may help you to talk to me. You see, I'm the publican of the New Liffey. A young lodger at my hotel, David Milligan, died cruelly on this very street last Sunday. I came here to see if I can find anything that might tell me who murdered him. I want the killer brought to justice.'

With a sob, the young woman stopped in her tracks, tears running down her face.

Judith said gently, 'My name is Judith—Mrs Judith Sampson. I'd be glad to know yours. Anything you say to me will be in confidence, I swear. If you were fond of David Milligan, I can tell you that I held him in respect and affection, and I want his murderer found.'

The shaky answer was, 'Jane. Jane Wilson.'

Two people walked past them at that moment and the young woman turned her head aside until they had passed. Seeing a bench further along the street, Judith kept her grip on the girl's arm and walked her along until they could both sit down.

So this was David's Jane! Judith's heart went out to her. 'I didn't mean to intrude on your troubles, Miss Wilson. But you looked ready to faint, back there. Will you let me help you?'

'Oh, it's so horrible, and I have no one to talk to about it. No one.'

Judith pressed her forearm, then let her go. 'Well, you have someone now. So, tell me what upsets you so much. Please. I won't be shocked, whatever you say. The truth will ease you. I really believe that.'

Chapter Five

Jane Wilson composed herself and looked at Judith. 'I'm sorry. Yes, I did know Mr Milligan. We saw each other more than once at St Philips church and, well, I thought he was a very nice young man. We were ... I was ...' She paused, obviously determined not to confess more. 'I expected to see him at church last Sunday but ... I read of his death in the paper.'

'It must have been an awful shock for you.'

'It was, Mrs Sampson. It was.'

'He was my lodger for no more than two months but I got to know him and thought well of him. A very nice young man, I agree, with a promising future. Tragic, for him to die like that.'

Jane pressed her lips together and nodded quickly.

Judith said, 'You attended the funeral, didn't you?'

Jane's eyes flashed at her. 'I didn't stay long. Just paid my respects and left.'

Judith admired the boldness and resolve that she could suddenly see in Miss Wilson. 'Will you tell me why you're here today?'

'I was visiting a friend,' Jane said, 'and thought I'd pass by here ... just to see.' She stood up and forced a smile. 'I must be on my way. Thank you, Mrs Sampson, for your time and your compassion. Goodbye.'

'Goodbye, Miss Wilson,' Judith said, and watched her go: a young woman in love, bowed down by sadness.

Judith opened her watch; there was no time to call at the Triumph, because she needed to be back at The Liffey. She walked away with the surname ringing in her head. *Wilson.* David had been going to meet 'Jane's father' that Saturday night because he had witnessed the man kill Peter Ryan. Well, that man's initials, written at the bottom of his own note, were TW. *T Wilson.* So this Mr Wilson was guilty of Ryan's death. What about that of David Milligan?

As soon as she returned to the Liffey, she confided in Michael. She began by telling him what she had found in David's room after he died.

'My God, you should have left it all there for the police! How else can they do their job?'

'I did. I left everything as it was. I only kept back the journal and the letters, for Milligan's sake and for the young lady's reputation. They're too personal and intimate. And they're of no use to the police because they don't name anyone to do with Peter Ryan's death. Besides, I left the paper that *did* name someone; it had the signature of the man that Milligan was supposed to meet at the Triumph, "TW". The police have that note and I hope they'll follow it up. And because of who I met today, I know the "W" stands for Wilson.'

'You've lost me,' Michael said. 'What have you been doing today?'

She told him about meeting Jane, which meant she had to explain who Jane was, and tell David Milligan's whole love story, which meant she also told him how their lodger had confided in her, more than a month before, about witnessing Ryan's death. 'You see why Milligan wasn't sure whether he should go to the police? And in the end of course he didn't, because he came to suspect the killer was Wilson.'

Judith rather expected to incur Michael's wrath over David Milligan's confidences, but to her relief she found her husband was more preoccupied about the identity of Jane's father. He pondered for a moment, then exclaimed, 'Thomas Wilson! Of course. A big trader in grain, known to our supplier; not sure where his warehouse is, but he lives on George Street. Has a son named Henry who's training up in the business, and a daughter whose name I don't know, but she's marriageable age, so that would fit.' He shook his head at Judith. 'My word, if he put paid to Ryan, he's even tougher and harder than his reputation makes out. Dangerous waters, my love, and you're best off leaving the police to navigate them.'

'You don't think I should take the information about Ryan to—?'

'Judith, Judith,' he said, taking her by the shoulders. 'You've done enough. More than enough. You're a good woman and a brave one, but information and evidence—they're for the police to sort out, if they can. There's two dead, yes, but that's two *men*. It's not a woman's sphere. It won't do us any good for you to meddle, my love. Trust me.'

Two days later, on Sunday 22 February, Judith and her family went on an outing to Governor's wharf, down at the bottom of Market Street. Judith had suggested it for good reason, though she hadn't shared that reason with Michael.

In the late morning, as they got near to Market Street, she was able to take a good look at the lampposts in Sussex Street. Just as she had expected, they passed by a vacant site with a stables at the back. On the street outside there was a lamppost that had clearly been damaged by a lightning strike: the top was split and askew, and one side was scorched. The original lamp had no doubt been smashed, because there was a new one attached nearer the ground. David's two descriptions of Peter Ryan's death, his verbal one to her, and the record in his journal, matched exactly. Judith said nothing about any of this to Michael, and they enjoyed a pleasant day.

On the following afternoon, Judith came into the bar and noticed her barman handing over a crate of bottled beer and two bottles of whisky to a sailor lad who stood in the doorway. He had a handcart outside, to take his purchases down to the *Cyprus*. Yes, of course. It was Captain Bates's lad from the *Cyprus* collecting an order. Judith had an idea. She went to the back of the bar, grabbed a blank piece of paper from her order book and started writing. She wanted to know from Captain Bates the whereabouts of his carpenter-mechanic … yes, Colin Smith … on the night of David's murder. She wrote down the date of that, Saturday 14 February. Bates had told her Smith held a grudge against David. 'Here,' she said giving the note to the lad. 'Take this to Captain Bates. I'd like his reply.'

The lad nodded and pocketed the paper. 'I'll be back in a few days for his next order. Can I bring it then? Will that be right?'

'That's all right.' Judith said and smiled. 'And don't drink any of that grog on the way back to the ship!'

'No, ma'am, no.' The lad took his load away. Judith watched him go and thought about the next man to investigate: Jack Prendergast, the aggressive gambler they'd banned from the New Liffey. He and Smith made two men with a grudge against David Milligan. And what about Thomas Wilson?

Three hours later on the same day, in the remaining sunlight of late summer, Anne Wilson and her husband were looking out into their rear garden, where their daughter Jane sat alone by the strawberry beds.

'I'm worried about her,' Anne said. 'Ever since that Sunday, when that American whaler didn't come to church, she hasn't been herself. And now we know he's dead. I feel as though she'll never smile again.'

'She'll get over it,' Thomas said. 'She's far better off never having to think about him again.'

'But for him to be murdered, Thomas. That's horrible. I can understand Jane's shock.'

'Sailors live risky lives,' Thomas said, 'and they die like flies. I don't want to talk about this any more.'

'Well, we have to do something about Jane. Perhaps a visit to the mountains might be best.'

'Perhaps,' Thomas said. 'Now, I must go. My businessmen's meeting is at York Street and I don't want to be late.'

Anne gave him a sharp look. 'These meetings of yours have been getting more and more frequent, Thomas, these last two months.'

'They're business and nothing else, Anne. If you wish, I'll collect a copy of the minutes for you to peruse.'

'There's no need for sarcasm. Just don't be late home tonight.'

Anne walked into the garden towards Jane, and Thomas left by the front door and headed up to Fort Street. On the way up the steep hill, he stopped to get his breath and gather his thoughts. It was now a week since the death of David Milligan, and Thomas felt he was back in control. His emotions had been powerful on the night when he did the deed. Anger had driven him to stab that young man, and for two days after, his remorse had almost overwhelmed him. Killing Ryan by accident had been a nightmare, but he had been able to banish it from his conscience. Milligan was another matter altogether. But he had reconciled himself to it since. He had done it to protect Jane and her future. Milligan would have told Jane anything to have his way with her. He was certain of that. No, his innocent and trusting daughter deserved to be saved from a man like that.

Thank God Jane was safe. There had been no gossip about her reckless meetings with the whaler. The sons of important people would soon be courting her; he knew through Henry that friends of the Campbells already admired her. And he, too, was safe from suspicion. He went over his movements on that night and was confident that no one had seen him in the act. His rapid exit from the Triumph hotel might have stayed in people's minds if the police went asking about who was drinking there that night, but he thought it was a low risk. Meanwhile, at the hotel in George Street where he drank after killing Milligan, he had made very sure he was seen by people he knew, and he'd made sure there were no bloodstains on him before he walked into the pub. So, a good alibi, he had that.

As for the sheath knife that he'd cast away in panic, it had preyed on his mind so much that he'd gone back two nights later and searched for it in the debris that always lay along the street. After five minutes, interrupted twice by people going by, he'd come up empty handed. Someone else had picked the knife up, and he just had to hope it wasn't the police. He gave a grim smile to himself: they'd never found any evidence to show who'd killed Ryan, so surely he could depend on their incompetence?

When he got to Fort Street he went straight to the brothel, nodded to the watchman and went inside.

Madame Greta greeted him with her usual knowing smile. 'Just passing, sir, or staying for a bit?'

'Might be looking for some company, perhaps.' A bright-headed woman lounging on a sofa looked at him wide-eyed for a second, then glanced away. He remembered her face, though not her name, because he'd seen her around Fort Street once or twice, as well as in the brothel. She must live in the neighbourhood. He'd never been attracted to her, so his eye slid over her and around the room, just as his favourite, Doreen, walked in.

Madame Greta noticed the direction of his hot glance, and beckoned the girl over to him. Doreen was smooth-skinned and with a ready laugh. A girl just out of puberty, still fresh and eager, or at least she pretended to be. And there she was in front of him. Just what he needed.

Madame smiled. 'Doreen is very popular tonight, but you're the one she fancies, sir. She'll take you upstairs for as long as you please.'

Lizzie stayed on the sofa and watched Thomas Wilson go with Doreen. It had been a shock to see him walk in and she hoped she hadn't betrayed that in her glance.

For the last week she had been worried that this man would turn up; a murderer whom she'd seen in the act, a murderer whose weapon she kept hidden in her room. She'd never told anyone and she'd never done anything about the frightful killing she'd watched in the dark. But here was the mongrel who'd done it, here and now. Thank goodness he hadn't chosen to put his hands on her! Pity poor Doreen.

Lizzie stood up, went to Madame's bar, tapped the shoulder of a well-dressed young man and gave him one of her best smiles. The young man's clear skin and blue eyes reminded her of the American whaler who'd bled to death in the street, not far away. Life was fragile. She felt relieved and sad at the same time when the young man grinned back.

* * *

Judith Sampson stepped out from behind the bar at the New Liffey on Tuesday night at eight pm. She told Michael she was going upstairs for some time to herself, but in fact she went out the side door into Cumberland Street. It was a warm evening and still light, and to her it felt like the last hurrah for summer. The streets were busy for a Tuesday: the people of The Rocks were out for pleasure and the bar at the New Liffey had been brisk and jolly. Death and disaster didn't seem to stay on people's minds for long. Sure, she had heard gossip and comments at the hotel about the murder of David Milligan, but they talked as if a dog had been skittled by a cart.

It made her angry, and she was going to talk to someone about it. TW. Mr Thomas Wilson. All she wanted was confirmation that he had met David Milligan in the Triumph hotel at his own invitation, on St Valentine's Day. And if she tackled him with this in front of his family, she believed he would have to tell her the truth.

Ten minutes later she was outside the front door of the Wilson house. She knocked and the door opened.

'Good evening, Mrs Wilson. I am Mrs Judith Sampson, licensee of the New Liffey hotel. Excuse the hour, and I'm sorry for not letting you know beforehand, but may I talk to your husband?'

Judith was surprised at the reaction she got from the woman: alarm, embarrassment, then confusion. Judith had the distinct feeling that Mrs Wilson was both suspicious and jealous of her—a compliment to Judith's looks, if not to her morals! Was Wilson unfaithful, and did his wife know it? Judith felt sorry for her, if so.

She kept her voice soothing and polite. 'I'm here in my capacity as licensee of the New Liffey, Mrs Wilson. No more.'

Mrs Wilson looked flustered, but less alarmed. 'On business? At this hour?'

'Publicans have no choice about the hours they keep. And I won't trouble you for long. My business is to do with one of our lodgers.'

Mrs Wilson stepped aside and nodded. 'My husband is in, Mrs Sampson. Please come through.'

Judith followed her into a well-furnished parlour, where Thomas Wilson was sitting on a sofa reading a newspaper. He stood up when Judith entered and looked at his wife with a question in his eyes. Judith at once recalled Milligan's description of the man who killed Ryan. *Early forties, five feet six inches, brown hair, curly, about fifteen stone.* God in heaven, this was the man.

'This is Mrs Sampson from the hotel, Thomas,' Anne said.

He frowned then he said, 'Mrs Sampson. How do you do?'

'I am in good health, thank you, Mr Wilson.'

'To what do we owe this visit? You're here about hops or barley?'

'No. An American whaler named David Milligan lodged at my hotel lately. Now that he's dead, I'll be corresponding with his parents. I'm speaking to people who saw him in his last days and I believe you are one of them. May I ask you some questions?'

Thomas Wilson's expression changed. He looked wary, annoyed, but not angry enough to say an outright no. He pressed his lips together and said nothing.

His wife covered up the awkward moment. 'Would you like to sit down, Mrs Sampson? May I offer you some refreshment?'

'Thank you, Mrs Wilson.' She sat down on a chair. 'But nothing to eat, thank you. As I came uninvited, I shall not take up too much of your time.' Judith sat with her back straight and waited until the Wilsons had sat down. 'Amongst David Milligan's effects at my hotel, I found a note from a gentleman who arranged to meet him at the Triumph hotel at nine o'clock on Saint Valentine's Day.' Wilson's eyes flickered at this and she knew she had hit the mark, so she ventured, 'That gentleman was yourself, sir. Can you tell me what happened at that meeting? I'm sure his poor parents would like to know. You were probably the last person to see David Milligan alive. Apart from his murderer, of course.'

Wilson's eyes were boring into hers. Was he fooled by her innocent tone, or did he think she suspected him? He looked at his wife, then back at Judith. If he denied the meeting, he might fear Judith would go to the law with the note. What was the lesser evil: answering her questions now or perhaps facing those of the police?

'Your question is an intrusion on the private life of my family, Mrs Sampson. I invited Milligan to the Triumph over something that he should have been ashamed of, and it will not edify his parents to hear of it. I will give you an answer, but my wife and I forbid you to share it with anyone else.' He turned from his wide-eyed spouse to glare at

Judith. 'I met Milligan to tell him once again that he was totally inappropriate as a suitor to my daughter. He had broken all rules of a well-mannered gentleman and I made it clear that he was to keep away from her.'

At that moment Jane Wilson appeared in the doorway of the parlour. She looked pale at what she had overheard, and addressed her father first. 'I didn't know you'd done that to David! How could you?' Then she looked at Judith, shivered and said, 'Good evening, Mrs Sampson!'

Wilson said in a harsh tone, 'I didn't tell you because it was between men. That whaler knew our views on his unsuitability. I repeated them, he heard them, and he left.'

'When was that exactly?' Judith said.

Wilson gave her an angry look. His self-control was slipping. 'I don't remember. It might have been eight-thirty, nine-thirty … No idea.'

Judith waited to see whether he would mention Milligan's death that night but the silence was interrupted by Jane, who was still standing at the doorway. She gave a little sob and tears were running down her face.

Her father said in a gruff voice, 'Jane, withdraw.'

Jane gave a nod to Judith. 'It's good to see you again, Mrs Sampson. I bid you good night.'

Wilson got to his feet and said to Judith, 'You've met my daughter before?'

Judith stood also, knowing she was well past her welcome in this house. 'Yes, a casual encounter while shopping.' She addressed herself to Mrs Wilson. 'Thank you for your time, Mrs Wilson. I'll be on my way.'

She ignored Thomas Wilson and went to the front door, which Mrs Wilson opened for her. She stepped onto the front verandah and turned to look at this decent-looking woman who, like her daughter, was living with a man whose tendency to violence was concealed. She and Jane might be due for a terrible shock one day.

Judith said, 'I got to know David Milligan quite well in the short time he stayed with us at the New Liffey. I am a simple woman from a simple background but I saw gifts and potential in that young man. For reasons unknown to us, his life was ripped from him in a horrible way. It is my goal to find out who killed him, and why.'

Mrs Wilson's eyes dimmed, and she recoiled a little. Tight-lipped, she said, 'I understand. Apart from the way he met Jane in secret, I knew no harm of him. You do what you must, to seek justice. Good evening.'

* * *

The next day at noon Judith made her way along Harrington Street towards the house where Jack Prendergast plied his trade; that was, when he made his mind up to work. Judith had known Helen Prendergast since before she had married Jack, and had watched the couple struggle over the years. Jack was a cabinetmaker and had set up his business in their back yard, but he was not a hard worker and kept people waiting for the things he made or repaired. His income was low in consequence and what was left from his perpetual gambling really only kept them in bread and vegetables. Helen and Jack sometimes lived on the high hog for a while, but then they'd be back scratching for pennies.

When Judith knocked on the door of the Prendergast's one-storey timber cottage, it was opened by a dark-haired woman, whose prematurely lined face broke into a smile, 'Morning to you, Judith. Come in. Come in.'

Judith stepped into their modest parlour. The curtains and ornaments were simple but clean, and the cabinetry was well made. 'How have you been, Helen?'

'Can't complain, love. We get by. If I had any troubles I'd be silly to share them: nobody would listen, especially in this town and especially where we live. Cup of tea?'

'If the kettle is on.'

'Always is. I won't be long.'

Judith took off her bonnet, sat down and thought about her confrontation with Thomas Wilson, the night before. Her instincts told her she had enough on him to go to the police and have him arrested for Ryan's murder. But she wasn't going to move against him yet. Not while there was a chance of finding out more about David's murder.

Helen came in with a tray carrying teapot and cups, and Judith was surprised to see Jack follow her in.

'Morning, Missus,' he said, concealing any grudges he might feel under a cheeky grin. 'Brought us some free beer, yeah?'

'G'day Jack,' she said. 'No, we give nothing away for free, you know that.'

Helen poured three cups and gave one to Judith. 'Things going all right at the pub? I heard about that poor lodger of yours. What a way to go, eh?'

Judith said at once, 'I want to find out who murdered him, Helen.'

Jack laughed. 'Good luck with that, Missus!'

Judith said, 'Last time anyone saw him was at the Triumph on the Saturday night, fourteenth of February. He was talking to Thomas Wilson, somewhere about eight or nine.' She looked at Jack, who was leaning against a sideboard, finishing off the tea before heading back out to the yard. 'I hear most of your card games are at the Triumph these days, Jack. Ten to one you were there that night. Did you notice Milligan? Did you speak with him at all?'

'He's the last mongrel I'd want to speak to, the way he cheated at every game! Yeah I saw him; glad to give him a wide berth, too.'

'So you saw him talking to Wilson. Did you notice when he left the Triumph?'

'Just a minute, just a bloody minute, Missus. You don't go interrogating *me* like that! You're no policeman, you're the woman who had me kicked out of the New Liffey for calling your precious lodger a cheat and a liar, which he was.'

'Give over, Jack,' Helen said. 'The young man's dead and that's no way to talk about him.'

Judith kept calm and said to the husband, 'Did he make you angry at the Triumph, Jack? Did you get your temper up?'

Helen shrank at those questions, and Judith worried that she'd gone too far. But Jack Prendergast gave her an answer, and despite her opinion of his character, she believed it.

'Never laid a hand on him. Yes I was at the pub that night, but I never went near him. He was flat out jawing away to Wilson, who didn't like what he was saying, I could see that. Wilson banged the table at one point and it looked like hammer and tongs between them, but they kept their voices low so I've no idea what it was about.'

Judith sipped more of her tea and put the cup down. 'Jack, I would really appreciate knowing, if you can tell me: what time did Milligan and Wilson leave the pub?'

Jack Prendergast gave a nasty laugh. 'What about me, first? Well, I got an alibi, Missus, and a good one. Ted Cruz was with me that night until late. A good customer of mine and a trusty. He will cover for me, for the whole time. I was in that bar until closing time, and I can tell you Milligan left the pub hours before I did. He'd only been gone minutes when Wilson left as well. Time of night? Not exactly sure, Missus, and you should be asking the barman at the Triumph, not me. Now, I'll be in the yard, Helen.' He left them.

Judith finished her tea. 'Thank you for the cup, Helen.'

'He's being straight with you,' Helen said, pouring her more tea. 'I know for a fact he was playing cards all that night at the Triumph. He never leaves a card table once he's settled in, more's the pity.'

'Thank you,' Judith said. She sighed. 'It looks more and more like Wilson was the last man to see David Milligan alive.'

Helen offered no remark on this and Judith changed the subject, asking Helen about her ageing relatives and her health. At the end of half an hour and more tea, Judith stood up. 'Thank you for the tea and chat. We must do this more often.' Jack walked in at that moment, so she turned to him and said, 'And thank you for the information, Jack. Is the Triumph your chosen watering hole now, or do you share yourself around?'

'I get around to a few pubs, Missus.' He winked. 'Inviting me back to the New Liffey?'

Judith picked up her bonnet. 'I'll let you back into the pub, Jack, as long as Helen here gives the go-ahead. Fair enough?'

Helen had her head down, hesitating. Before she could say anything, Jack put his hand up in a half-wave to Judith. 'Gotta get back to work. See you, Missus.'

'Goodbye, Jack.'

Helen saw Judith out. On the doorstep, she said in a low voice, 'He is still the same, Judith. No better and no worse. This is what God has given me, and I have to put up with it. Goodbye, and don't let this make you a stranger.'

'I won't. See you, Helen.'

*　*　*

Just before the pub opened the next day, Judith was sweeping the footpath when she spotted the *Cyprus* lad pulling a handcart along Cumberland Street towards her. 'Good morning. Here for more of our great beer?'

'Yes, ma'am.' He brought out a piece of paper from his trousers. 'Captain Bates told me to give you this.'

'Thank you.' Judith took the note and read it. Bates gave her his compliments of the day and went on to say where carpenter Colin Smith had been on the afternoon and night of 14 February. He had spent all day and part of the evening with a labouring party, completing the timber work to the damaged hull. That work was finished about ten o'clock and Captain Bates himself had inspected it. Colin Smith had not left the ship that night.

Judith put the note away and said to the boy, 'Please thank the captain for this when you get back. Now, follow me and we'll fix you up.'

Judith opened the pub, let in the young whaler and closed the door behind her. As she got the beer and spirits, she crossed both

Colin Smith and Jack Prendergast from her mental list of possible killers. She was doing the police's work for them over the murder of David Milligan. When should she go to them about Thomas Wilson— did she have enough to convince them?

Judith added an extra two bottles of beer to the consignment. 'A present for your Captain. Make sure he knows they're free from me.' The lad knuckled his forehead in response.

Half an hour later the pub was open and Judith was upstairs, arranging new bed linen. Towards noon, Michael came up and hung around talking as she worked, without getting much response.

'Are you all right, love?'

Judith looked at him surprised. 'Of course. Why do you ask?'

'Because you've got too much on your mind. Every other night you're restless in bed. I know what it is: you're worked up about Milligan's death and who killed him. But I don't know what you expect to achieve, questioning neighbours and our friends about him.'

'I'm gathering facts, Michael. And I'm not going to let it alone, so don't try to discourage me.'

He considered her and said, a little surprised, 'You really are on the scent, aren't you?'

'Well, someone has to be. I bet London to a brick if I went to the police station now, David's file would be lying dusty at the bottom of the pile. I'm doing no more than the constables should be doing. And I'm getting closer to the culprit.'

'Oh, aye, and who might that be?'

'I'll tell you when I'm certain; it won't be long now.'

'Well just don't let it eat you up, dear. We have enough to do around here without you worrying about this all the time.'

Judith put her hands on her hips. 'Have our meals been poor? Are we losing money? Is the hotel unclean? Are the children dirty?'

Michael laughed, which increased her irritation, then said, 'No, of course not. None of that is true.' Before she could resist, he pulled her close and held her. 'It's just that I don't want to see you upset about all this.'

She gave him a half smile and he let her go. 'I'm not upset and I'm making progress.'

He grimaced. 'All right, what about the other death? Ryan's? Any closer to knowing who might have put him in a box?'

'You know what, Michael, I think David Milligan's murder and the murder of Peter Ryan are connected somehow.'

'My goodness,' Michael said. 'You really are onto something aren't you?' He gave her a concerned look. 'Look, I can put up with your sleuthing, but only if you promise not to do anything dangerous.'

'My dear, it's not like that. It's more like doing a jigsaw. I haven't seen the whole picture yet but I'm starting to. Let me get back to my duties.'

He pecked her on the cheek. 'Done. I'll make a lunch for us in half an hour.'

'Good man.'

* * *

Thomas Wilson was bored and restless. It was Friday night, and he was at a gathering of the St Philip's parish committee. There were a dozen couples in the hall located next to St Philips church, mingling after their fundraising meeting. There wasn't a bottle of whisky or beer in sight, and he had to put up with tea and cakes. He'd love to be able to duck out to Fort Street for some relaxation. Right now, he was sitting with Anne, who was in conversation with the minister. The couple beside the minister were a dull lot but thankfully Thomas was on the end of the row, sitting in silence. His mind wandered.

There was some scuttlebutt going around town about Milligan's murder. Not much, just someone enquiring about who was where on the night of St Valentine's Day. It wasn't the coppers; he had an easy-going relationship with the sergeant at The Rocks police station, who had told him that Milligan's murder was well down on their list of priorities. So, who was delving into this? Apart, of course, from that woman publican who had been at his house the other night with her damned impudent questions.

He went cold every time he remembered Judith Sampson's claim that she had seen the note to Milligan, summoning the whaler to the Triumph. But he'd printed the lines, not done them in longhand, and only signed the note 'TW'. Even suppose the police had that note, what could they make of it? There were plenty of men in Sydney with the initials TW. Who was to say the 'W' didn't stand for Wentworth, for instance? The notorious D'Arcy Wentworth had no legitimate child with the initial 'T', but there were a few by-blows … Wilson smiled cynically to himself.

Ted Cruz pulled a chair up beside him and Wilson turned to him politely. The man had a few quid, plus acreage near the Macarthurs' property and an office in town. 'So, saw you at the Triumph on Valentine's Day, Wilson. You didn't stay long; eager to head home to the comely Mrs Wilson?' Cruz nodded to Anne, but she was talking across the minister to the couple on the other side.

Thomas was startled; he hadn't noticed Cruz that night. Too obsessed with trying to handle Milligan, and look how that ended. No good denying it, because Cruz had an excellent memory for facts and it would be sensible to find out what else he'd seen. 'Yes, I was there.' Wilson lowered his voice. 'I had to give a lad a dressing down. American whaler; you might've noticed him outside the church just before Christmas. Typical Yankee: he thought he could just talk to my daughter without an introduction. That night I chipped him about it, good and proper.'

Cruz nodded. 'It got heated at one stage. Saw you hitting the table.'

'The young rogue wouldn't be told, Ted,' Wilson said. 'But I think he got the message in the end.'

Ted drank the rest of his cup of tea. 'They're a brash lot, the whalers, not to mention violent. I'm not surprised that one got his come-uppance. Mind you, the publicans at the New Liffey reckon he was next thing to an angel.' He shook his head. 'I was at Jack Prendergast's this morning, giving him the final order for my cabinets. He said that Mrs Sampson was over his place the other day saying the police aren't doing enough and there has to be evidence to prove who killed Milligan, and she's out to find it. She's got every excuse to cry him up, I suppose; he was her lodger, after all. But damn it, he was just a bleeding sailor! I must be off. Nice to talk to you, Wilson.'

Wilson watched him go and went cold again. He'd have to do something about Judith Sampson.

* * *

On the following day, Saturday, in the afternoon, Michael Sampson was in a heated conversation with Thomas Wilson in the New Liffey bar, which he interrupted by drawing the man into his office, away from his patrons' ears.

'Sit down, please,' Michael said, sitting down opposite the barley wholesaler and coming straight to the point. 'David Milligan was a lodger, Mr Wilson, under our roof for almost two months. He was a nice young bloke, and his death was tragic. My wife has every right to find out how he died; in fact the police have asked her to pass on anything new that we happen to hear about him. She is not spreading gossip and she is not giving you a bad name. She is just doing her job.'

'Her job is here, Sampson. Her job is to run this pub, not to slander and malign me right through The Rocks and beyond.'

Michael Sampson laughed. 'What rot, sir. She's done nothing of the kind. She's a respectable woman who's willing to assist the police. They have a lot on their hands; sailors' deaths in this town are as common as the mud on your boots.'

Thomas Wilson stood up. 'I'm warning you, Sampson. Your wife will cease asking about my whereabouts and what I do. If I hear any more of her nonsense, there will be consequences.'

'What do you mean, sir?'

'If your wife keeps meddling in matters that are no concern of hers, and utters slander about me, then I'll make sure no one supplies grain for brewing to this hotel in the future. Do you understand now?'

Michael considered this, but only for a moment. He did not doubt Wilson's power to place hurdles in the way of produce being supplied to the New Liffey, but the man did not have a monopoly on the trade. 'That's a despicable threat, Wilson, and I want you out of my pub.'

Wilson turned to leave and looked back at him. 'Just mind what I say and keep your wife under control.' He left the office.

* * *

Judith Sampson was going to see Elsie Ryan, on the same Saturday. Her house was in Pitt Street, a modest bungalow. Judith had not met the ticket-of-leave woman in over a year. Michael and Judith had never dealt with Peter Ryan because they thought him underhanded in business, but his wife had always been pleasant and nice to Judith.

'Good afternoon, Elsie,' Judith said to the tall, middle-aged woman who opened the door.

'Good to see you, Judith,' Elsie said. 'Come in.' She led Judith into the parlour and offered her a chair.

'First of all,' Judith said, 'I've come to give both Michael's and my own condolences on your husband's death. I haven't seen you since, and I wondered how you're going.'

Elsie nodded. 'Thank you. It's still tough. Can I get you something to drink?'

'No, thank you. Not just yet. It must be terrible for you, waiting for the police to find out what happened. Have they made any progress? Have they been of any help to you?'

Elsie's face became hard, masking her sadness. 'They keep asking around about what they call Peter's movements that night, but they won't listen to *me*, his own wife! He left from here to go to a meeting that night, and I know where it was and who was meeting him. It was in the very spot where Peter died, and the man who wanted to meet him there was Thomas Wilson.'

Judith started. 'Are you certain?'

'That's what the police asked me,' Elsie cried, 'and I told them, certain sure. I saw the note from Wilson, and Peter had it in his pocket when he left this house to go to Sussex Street.'

'A note?' Judith said, thinking instantly of the document she had hidden away at the New Liffey, amongst David Milligan's things. 'That's evidence, then.'

'I told the police that,' Elsie said, 'but they said that it wasn't found on his … body.' Elsie forced her lips against each other and blinked.

Judith looked at her with compassion. 'If this is too much …'

'No, Judith, it helps me to talk about it. Wilson wanted Peter to pay a ridiculous price for the barley he supplied him, I told the police that, too. I knew that's what they'd be talking about at Sussex Street—after hours and in the dark, what's more. What were we to make of that? But the police told me I didn't have evidence who Peter met, and it's just *hearsay!*' Elsie put her hands over her face and said the word as though it were an insult.

Judith felt for her. 'Evidence from a man's wife doesn't seem to weigh much with the police. They think we're biased, one way or the other. But they should have questioned Wilson by now. Do you know if they have?'

'Yes, I asked because it's my right. I went to the station and asked to see the sergeant. He told me Wilson was never at Sussex Street, he was somewhere else that night. I said about the note again and he said *hearsay.*'

Judith leaned forward. Damn it, the police had that note; she'd left it in the drawer for them to find! 'Elsie, what if I could find that note?'

Elsie Ryan looked at her in amazement. 'What do you mean? How on earth—?'

'Thomas Wilson has been threatening us lately because I've been trying to discover who murdered our lodger, David Milligan. I've been digging into Thomas Wilson's movements, as the police call them, over the last two months, and I don't like what I've found.'

'You've found the *note?*'

'I'm not going to tell you any more, Elsie, until I think there could be a case—or maybe two—against that man. Please don't get your hopes up. Knowing the police and the magistrates in this town, who can say whether he'll ever go to trial? But I want to try. Your husband needs justice, and maybe I'm the person chosen to help you get that. If I find more evidence against Wilson, they'll have to arrest him and bring him to trial. So they'll call you as a witness for the Crown, and they'll have to listen to you in court. Can you do that, stand up before a jury in public while they ask you about Peter, and that night, and what you know?'

'I'll do anything to get Peter's killer. Oh, I know he had a bad name in certain parts and he did the wrong thing in business now and then. But he didn't deserve to get killed.'

'No, he did not. Leave it with me.' Judith sat back and smiled. 'Now, it has been too long since we last met. I'll have that cuppa, and if it's not too much trouble, please tell me what you've been doing and how your family is going.'

'It's no trouble at all and I welcome it. Let me put the kettle on and I'll be right back.'

As Elsie left the room, her step lighter, Judith made a decision. In her mind, Thomas Wilson had killed both Peter Ryan and David Milligan. He would hang for either crime, and the strongest case against him was the murder of Peter Ryan. If she could possibly accomplish it, Wilson would hang for murder, and David Milligan would be avenged.

There would be nasty things come out of this in the meantime, including Wilson cutting off the supply of barley and malt to the New Liffey. That they would face. She and Michael together.

* * *

On the Monday morning next, before the pub had opened, Judith was standing in the foyer of The Rocks police station, opposite the two policemen who had come to her hotel soon after Peter Ryan's death. The taller one was Constable Martin and the other Constable Walsh. Judith had asked to see their superior officer but he was not at the station, and nor was the sergeant whom Elsie Ryan had mentioned.

115

Laid out on the counter between Judith and the constables was a document with her name, address and the number of her hotel license. Beside it was David Milligan's journal. Judith had not brought Jane Wilson's love letters with her—that innocent young woman was about to be exposed to horror and scandal already because of her father's attack on Ryan; she did not deserve to have her love life exposed as well.

Judith and Michael had decided that she should come alone to put this evidence before the police. If they both went, it might look as though they were cooking up accusations to counter Wilson's threats against the New Liffey. Judith felt quite capable of fronting up alone this morning, but she was grateful that at this early hour there was no one else in the foyer of the station.

She looked hard at Constable Martin. 'I'll be back tomorrow morning to speak to your superior and make a proper deposition. But I'm glad to have brought this evidence at once, because I know how important it is in the Peter Ryan case.'

Walsh's eyes widened. 'Really? And you say you just found this journal, Mrs Sampson?'

'Over the weekend. It had fallen behind a piece of furniture in the room that used to be occupied by David Milligan. It was lucky I found it.'

'Indeed,' Martin said. 'But you are sure it's Milligan's? There's no name within it.'

'If you look under the clasp, you can see his initials.'

Walsh opened the journal. 'So I see.' He started scanning the journal and Judith said to Constable Walsh, 'Most of his diary is about a young woman called Jane—there's no other name for her and I hope the police can keep all that private. The most important part is where Milligan writes about the killing of Peter Ryan. All the details are there. The whole incident is described: the storm, the argument between the two men, the lightning strike on the lamppost, and then the description of the man who killed Ryan.'

Judith glanced back at Constable Martin, who by his fixed gaze looked as though he was reading those very pages. Judith said to him,

116

'And later on you'll see that Milligan recognised the same man in the flesh, much later. He is Thomas Wilson.'

Martin looked up. 'This is a dead man's testimony. Milligan is not around to verify it. He can't stand as a witness.'

'You can take *my* word, *and* his captain's, that he was an honest man and everything he wrote there is the truth! And you can call me as a witness: David Milligan confided in me about that night and he was debating whether to come to you and denounce Wilson. He was killed before he could do so.'

'With respect, that's hearsay, Mrs Sampson.'

'And there's the note, plain as plain! You've had that note ever since you got David Milligan's effects from his room in the New Liffey. Thomas Wilson's request to meet Peter Ryan on Sussex Street. When you get his file and take another look at it, you'll see it's stained by rainwater from the storm. But it's signed.'

Martin looked disconcerted. Judith could see that her first skirmish had influenced both constables, so she decided to retreat for now, and go on the attack again when she saw their superior next day.

'Right,' Martin said. 'Thank you for this. We'll write up a report.'

'I need a receipt for that journal,' Judith said. She pulled out a piece of paper from her bag. 'There's a copy of the note here, as far as I can remember it, and a description of the journal and its contents. Please sign and date it.'

Martin glanced at his offsider, then took a pen out of the inkwell in front of him and did as he was asked. He put the pen back in the inkwell, shook the paper to dry it, and handed it to Judith with a slight bow. 'Thank you, ma'am. I shall inform the superintendent to expect you tomorrow. Good day to you.'

* * *

It was Monday 3 May and chilly for autumn, so Lizzie Robinson was wearing her shawl. She was in the back row of the public gallery of the criminal court and she'd come every day so far. The courthouse was packed because the jury was 'out' but they were expected back after being been locked up for two days thinking about their verdict. Lizzie couldn't see why they had to think so long about it and hoped they'd make up their minds this afternoon. She'd been paying attention to this trial of Mr Thomas Wilson. It wasn't the trial for the murder she'd seen, when that poor young man was knifed on Fort Street. It was for the murder of Peter Ryan. But the murderer was the same man, and if he was called 'Guilty' by this jury, she'd feel like leaping up on her seat and screaming out the word herself.

But this wasn't the trial over David Milligan so she hadn't had to do or say anything. It had all been down to Judith Sampson's guts in going to the coppers and getting him charged. Lizzie could have been a witness to David Milligan's murder but it would have scared the shit out of her. Instead, Wilson would hang for Ryan's, so she didn't have to name nobody, go into the witness stand, give a statement. No, nothing. Wilson would go down for Ryan's murder. All the women at the brothel were convinced about that, and thrilled.

Lizzie felt like an expert after all these days at the court, even though some of the speeches and arguments didn't make much sense to her. What she could work out was that the sailor, David Milligan, had been an eyewitness to the fight between Ryan and Wilson. His diary was the key thing against Wilson. And there was a note that Wilson had signed—or at least there were three letters on it, 'Wil' because it had got wet in the rain. So that put Wilson at the scene of the crime. And surely Wilson had killed Ryan 'beyond reasonable doubt'.

Yes, Milligan wasn't alive to testify, but his diary was damning, especially the note. Of course there was no live eyewitness to the murder, only the word of a dead man, and a sailor to boot. So that was the weak bit, and the defending lawyer said the evidence was Sir Constanshul. Whoever that was, Lizzie thought the evidence sounded very clear when that part of the diary was read out. And the wife of Peter Ryan, who'd burst into tears on the stand when she talked about the same night, said Thomas Wilson was a monster, though the judge said that word had to be struck out.

The Crown had been very good in its attack on Wilson, and Lizzie thought the jury would find him guilty. Once a guilty verdict was brought down, she could sleep easy, knowing that Wilson would hang or at least be locked up for a long time.

There was commotion around her, and she realised that the jury had returned. They went through some rigmarole that Lizzie didn't understand. Then the judge called for silence, and he looked at the note that the foreman had given him. The judge addressed the jury. 'How do you find the accused, guilty or not guilty?'

This was the moment Lizzie had been waiting for and she held her breath.

'Not guilty, Your Honour.'

The judge nodded, picked up his gavel and banged it on a piece of wood. 'The jury is discharged. The accused is free to leave.'

Lizzie gasped and sat back in a daze. Everyone around her, a lot of whom she recognised from The Rocks, must have been thinking the way she had, because there was a kind of growling noise all along the gallery. The mongrel had got away with it.

Dismay flooded through her. He'd got away with murder. David Milligan was dead. Peter Ryan was dead. And the man who had killed them both was alive and free. Lizzie left the courthouse at once without talking to anyone and made her way to Fort Street. Along the streets, images vacillated in her mind. Every now and then, the innocent face of that American whaler appeared to her.

She went straight to the brothel, though it wasn't time for work yet. She needed people around her. She needed to be in a place where Thomas Wilson would never set foot again, because Madame Greta had banned him. Lizzie wished she could change everything back to the way it should be—but she just sat on the bed in her room, trembling. She didn't have Judith Sampson's courage.

* * *

119

Judith's spirits plummeted as she saw the gloating face of Thomas Wilson approach the bar at the New Liffey. She was prepared for him, because she and Michael and had talked through their strategy, on the night after Wilson was pronounced a free man.

'Good morning, Mrs Sampson,' Wilson said. 'I'd like to see you and your husband—now.'

Judith caught Michael's eye on the other side of the bar room, and beckoned to him. 'Good morning, Mr Wilson. Come with me.'

When the three of them were in the small office, Michael Sampson closed the door and remained standing. He did not offer Wilson a chair.

'I'll come right to the point,' Wilson said. 'I am innocent of Peter Ryan's murder—'

'You were found not guilty, sir,' Michael said quietly. 'There's a difference.'

'There you go again!' Wilson exclaimed. 'You two have flung enough mud at me, especially you, Mrs Sampson. I told you before I will not let you get away with this. I could have you up for slander, but I don't see why I should go to the expense. So get this: from the end of the month, you will not get your supplies from any barley retailer in this town. I control six of them and the rest know well that if they treat with you, they will have me to deal with.' He stood back with his arms folded.

'You cannot strangle our business,' Judith said. But she knew he could, if his fellow traders were sufficiently intimidated by him.

'You take it up with your lawyers if you wish. Good luck with that. Just remember I can issue a writ against you and this hotel for what you've done to me and my family.'

Judith said, 'It's what you've already done, Mr Wilson, that disgusts me.'

Wilson was red-faced. 'Blast you, woman! You never seem to learn.'

Michael opened the door of the office. 'Go.'

Wilson strode out. Judith sat down and so did Michael.

'We knew it would come to this,' Judith said. 'In a month or so we'll take a hit to our profits. Have to tighten the belt here and there. Meanwhile, my dear, better get on that horse and find us a new supplier.'

'Righto, then,' he said. 'I'll head straight for Toongabbie. There'll be farmers out there who don't like Wilson any more than we do. Will you be all right for a few days here, while I get us out of this mess?'

Judith forced a smile. Michael had shown his usual steadfastness and kindness with her, ever since Wilson's trial. Yet their present situation was all her fault. If she hadn't meddled in the murder investigation, they would not be in this fix. She loved her husband for standing by her. 'I'll be all right, dear. On your way.'

Michael left the office. Judith leaned her elbows on the desk and put her head in her hands. At the trial, the witnesses' testimony against Wilson had been called 'hearsay' by the defence. Judith herself had not been called, but the Crown had quoted the diary and the note, all the evidence that she thought would convict Wilson for sure … But the defence said it was 'circumstantial'. She felt defeated. David Milligan's voice, her voice, Elsie Ryan's: in the end they counted for nothing.

* * *

Two days later, with Michael still away, Judith was doing their books in the office behind the bar. It had been a depressing hour of working out where they could cut costs, including sacking one of their barmen. If they put these measures in place soon, the pub would survive, but only just.

A barman poked his head into the office. 'Someone to see you, Missus, outside. She said she wouldn't come in.'

Judith sighed and closed the ledgers. She walked to the front door, noting how few clients were in the bar. Word had got around already that the Sampsons were in strife. The faces looking at her now were loyal, but she could not rely on those good people alone for future income. Judith looked outside and saw a woman with a shawl waiting outside with a basket over her arm. On seeing Judith she came no closer, so Judith went up to her.

The woman said in a quiet voice, 'Do you have a side entrance?'

Judith was surprised but said, 'Follow me.'

At the entrance further down Cumberland Street, she beckoned the woman inside. She was in her twenties, pretty but a bit worn and faded, with dark hair and worried eyes. She looked somehow familiar. 'Do I know you?' Judith asked, as they went down the passage to the office.

The woman paused at the door of the office as though afraid to enter. 'Thank you for seeing me, Mrs Sampson. I'm Lizzie Robinson. I didn't want to talk outside because I didn't think you'd want to be seen with me. I work at Fort Street at Madame Greta's.' She shrank against the doorpost, anticipating rejection.

Judith gestured for her to go in. 'Please sit down. I've heard of Madame Greta's. In my pub, I think I've seen one or two of the women who work with you. It's a tough job that you do and I'm not judging anyone. As long as people behave themselves in my bar room.'

Lizzie went into the office, put her shopping basket on the floor and sat down. Judith sat behind the desk and waited for the girl to speak.

Lizzie's eyes softened. 'You're a good woman, Mrs Sampson. You don't look down on us girls. That's why I came to you. You see, I heard you brought that Wilson to trial—'

'It was the police and the Crown that did that.'

'But everyone says you were the one as chased that mongrel down for them! That took some guts, that did. That gave me gumption to come to you today. But you have to help me, Mrs Sampson; you gunna have to hold my hand all the way, because what I have to tell you is gunna put me in danger. Will you help me?'

Judith was startled. 'I might be able to help you, but you'll have to tell me what your problem is, first.'

'I want you just to listen to start with. Because if you don't, nobody else will.' Lizzie Robinson sucked in a deep breath and let it out. 'I saw Thomas Wilson kill David Milligan.'

Judith was thankful she was seated, because if she hadn't been, she would have fallen over. 'What did you say?'

'I was at the Triumph buying some gin. I saw Wilson and the American arguing. I paid for the gin and went to my place, to leave the bottle before I went to work. I looked through my curtains and I saw the American come by and stop and lean against a wall, and then I saw Wilson come up and stab him. Right there in the street, just yards from my front door. I was so shocked, Mrs Sampson, you got no idea, near pissed myself. Sorry.'

Judith shook her head. 'That's quite all right, Lizzie. Can I call you Lizzie?'

'Of course you can.'

'When Wilson got taken to court because of what he did to Ryan, I thought he'd hang. I thought all this would be over. But it ain't. I've had trouble eating and sleeping, Missus. I liked that young American.'

'That makes two of us, Lizzie. Does Wilson know you saw him kill David Milligan?'

'No, no!'

'And you didn't think of going to the police?"

'*Me*. With the job I do? That's a laugh,' Lizzie said miserably. 'It would have been just my word as a whore against him as a gentleman.'

'He's no gentleman, Lizzie. He might have got away with murdering Ryan, but the trial has put a huge dent in his reputation. If he were accused of Milligan's murder, I don't think a soul in Sydney would believe him innocent. If only we had good evidence to prove it.'

'That's what I thought,' Lizzie said. 'It's no good if I got nothin' but my word. But if I'd got nothin' I wouldn't have come to see you. Look at this.' To Judith's surprise, she lifted her basket up onto the desk and took out something wrapped in a cloth. 'I've got evidence, Mrs Sampson. Something to make Wilson dance on a rope.' Inside the cloth was a folded newspaper. She opened this up and Judith gasped.

'This is the knife that killed Milligan. If you look close, you'll see it's got Wilson's initials on it.'

Judith looked down in horror. Sure enough, 'TW' was engraved near the hilt, on the blood-covered steel. An expensive sheath knife, bought by a trader who liked to swagger it amongst the grain growers up country.

Lizzie said, 'I saw him use this. He threw it away but I got it back afterwards, because I couldn't bear what he'd done. I didn't show it to the police because I was scared, but I won't be if you come with me. So, will you help?'

Judith put out her hand and clasped Lizzie's free one. 'You saw David die. Was it ... was it quick?'

Lizzie lowered her head and dropped the knife onto the newspaper, remembering. 'He lived a minute or two. Long enough to say something to me. A woman's name. Jane Wilson.' She gazed at Judith, puzzled. 'Doesn't Wilson have a daughter called Jane?'

Judith nodded, sickened but with her mind whirling. The Crown had quoted from David Milligan's journal at the trial, but only the passages relating to Peter Ryan; they had suppressed any references to the love story contained in its pages, so as not to diminish Milligan's standing in the eyes of the jury. David had been presented as a decent man of good character and his illicit meetings with Jane had not been raised.

'Yes, Wilson does have a daughter called Jane. And she and her mother are about to face a tragedy they cannot avoid.' She stood up. 'I'll go with you to The Rocks police, Miss Lizzie Robinson, and they'll have to listen to us. That knife is evidence and it's certain to be verified as such. The police will find the maker that Wilson ordered it from, the blood will be identified as human, and you'll testify that it was used on Milligan. There were no other murders in Sydney town that night. The blood on this knife is Milligan's. And the initials on it are Wilson's.'

In October of the year 1824, Lizzie Robinson, Michael and Judith Sampson were amongst a crowd of people, some of them boisterous and many of them drunk, as they watched a man climb the scaffold to be hanged by the neck until dead, for the murder of David Milligan of Massachusetts, late carpenter-mechanic on the whaling ship, *Cyprus*.

The scaffold had been set up in the hanging place, a scrubby section between Castlereagh and Elizabeth Streets. Like blood sports and dockyard brawls, the hanging place was a source of entertainment for some of the inhabitants of Sydney Cove and The Rocks. But the Sampsons, the captain and crew of the *Cyprus* and many other spectators were not there for fun, and nor were women like Elsie Ryan or Lizzie Robinson.

Judith was there to see justice done. She was there in the hope that the soul of David Milligan could now rest in peace. There was no joy in her feeling of achievement. No pride in getting Wilson convicted. Just a sense that she had done what she had to do, from the moment she'd found David's journal in his hotel room. It was as if a spirit had directed her investigations, from that day to this final reckoning.

While a minister stood beside the very subdued Thomas Wilson and said something to him, Judith threw a glance at the family. The son's face was defiant, the mother was weeping and the daughter, Jane, was just staring ahead in shock. That was where the real tragedy lay. Wilson would hang, his body would rot, his spirit would be judged by God, but he left behind a living, grieving family and a broken-hearted young woman. It was a cruel and bad day.

The trapdoor banged open and Judith started at the sound. She forced herself to see Wilson drop, and did not look away until she knew he was no more.

She turned to Michael. 'Come, my dear, let's leave this place and get back to our lives.'

More Books by the Author

Unbound Justice (The Australian Sandstone Series Book 1)
Unshackled (The Australian Sandstone Series Book 2)
Succession (The Australian Sandstone Series Book 3)
Bailed Up (The Australian Sandstone Series Book 4)

Unbound Justice

The Australian Sandstone Series Book 1

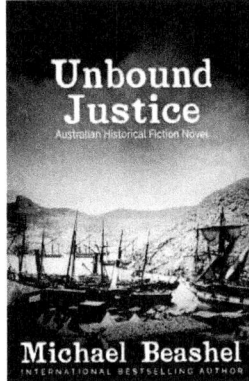

John Leary boards ship in Ireland in 1850, a young immigrant carpenter ambitious for a new life in Australia. He sails with revenge in his heart--his beloved sister has been raped by her landlord, William Baxterhouse, who escapes on another ship with even grander plans for success in New South Wales. In Sydney, hard workers like Leary and ruthless newcomers like Baxterhouse find a city fired by the Gold Rush and dedicated to creating the finest buildings in the colony.

Leary has a double motive to make his construction company succeed: he has fallen in love with the beautiful Clarissa McGuire, whose family despise him, and Baxterhouse continues to rise in wealth and influence, seemingly untouchable. Meanwhile another woman, Beth O'Hare, is in love with John Leary, and he makes some hard choices--including a climactic showdown with Baxterhouse.

Unbound Justice is now available on Amazon in ebook and paperback

Unshackled

The Australian Sandstone Series Book 2

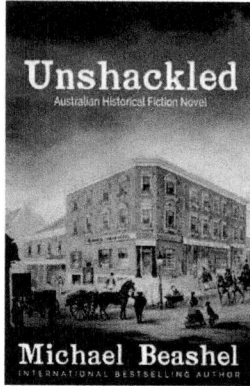

Sydney is booming in 1855 and life looks grand for John Leary: his construction dreams are coming true, his beloved wife Clarissa is expecting their first child and, with his partner Sean Connaire, he has produced some of the city's significant buildings. But success provokes jealousy, and a mysterious rival sabotages a vital Leary site.

John Leary cannot control his own company while his father-in-law holds a majority share, so he arranges a buyout on his own behalf--but this new, silent partner poses a serious risk to the harmony of his marriage. Meanwhile ex-convict Gerry Gleeson makes himself known to John as his uncle and helps him track down the saboteur.

Raw ambition, guilty secrets and undercover deals--will they bring the young builder to ruin or triumph?

Unshackled is now available on Amazon in ebook and paperback

Succession

The Australian Sandstone Series Book 3

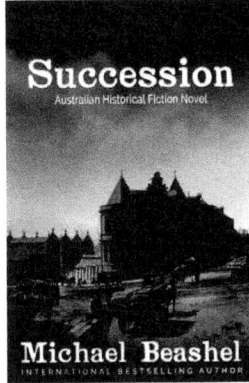

Leary Contracting has to build it--the tallest hotel Sydney has ever seen. At 55, John Leary employs both his sons in his construction company, but the one he favours is his first-born, Richard. Meanwhile Richard's half-brother, Brendan, gains the respect of the Leary workers because he has 'bricks in his blood'.

John begins the massive hotel project, overcoming city red tape and the jabs of his fiercest competitor. The Imperial dwarfs all around it, with hundreds of workers busting their guts to finish the brutal program. Richard, charming but unreliable, marries well and dazzles the Sydney society of 1885, while Brendan proves himself tougher than he looks whenever real work is required.

John must choose which of his sons will lead Learys into the next century. Only after the Imperial is completed does he make his decision. Succession is the third Australian Historical Fiction novel in The Australian Sandstone Series, a magnificent view of 19c Sydney from the ground up!

Succession is now available on Amazon in ebook and paperback

Bailed Up

The Australian Sandstone Series Book 4

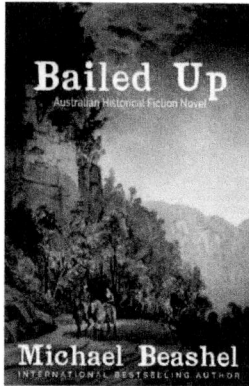

To Irishman Gerry Riordan, a pint at the Drawbridge Hotel in Cork makes the ideal end to the working week, and one winter night in 1828 he has good reason to celebrate with his friend, Lawrence Toole—Gerry is now a certified stonemason. Next day he will deliver gold tabernacle doors to St Mary's Cathedral and dare to ask the beautiful Anne Donovan to marry him.

But by the next night the gold has been stolen, Lawrence Toole lies dead and Riordan is accused of theft and murder. Anne, his boss's daughter, is the only person who believes him innocent.

Riordan escapes hanging but is transported to New South Wales. A convict in irons, with a flaming temper, he is forced to labour on the colony's toughest project, the Great North Road. As he begins working in stone again, a charming young woman, an enigmatic overseer and two convict friends seek to open his eyes to a more promising future. Meanwhile, offenders who framed him for the crimes in Ireland are also in the colony. Is there really any hope for Gerry Riordan to rebuild his shattered dreams?

Bailed Up is now available on Amazon in ebook and paperback

The Author

Born in Sydney, Michael Beashel is an International Bestselling Author. His Irish forebears immigrated to New South Wales in the 1860s and settled in Miller's Point. He spent his youth in Bondi, is married with adult children and lives in Sydney's inner-west.

Beashel was head of Asset Development for a global accommodation services company registered on the NYSE and has made his mark in some of Australia's iconic construction companies. In Sydney, he has restored government buildings such as the Customs House and the Town Hall and completed commercial buildings in the private sector. In SE Asia, he managed a construction division that built apartments and hotels in Bangkok and Ho Chi Minh City.

This industry—its characters, clients, tradespeople, designers and bureaucrats—provides rich material for his writing. He has an eye for the emergence of Sydney's built form, from the early days of the colony to the present, and a love of construction. He says about his writing, 'It's a passion. I revel in using the building industry as a tapestry to weave a great tale seasoned with historic facts and memorable characters. Human shelter is an essential need and I suspect people have a fascination for understanding its context and construction within their societies. Australia still is a young country in terms of large structures but there are many, many outstanding building stories.'

Beashel holds a B. App. Science (Building) from Sydney's UTS and is a member of Writing NSW. *Unbound Justice* is his first novel and Books 2 and 3 *Unshackled* and *Succession* form the first three of The Australian Sandstone Series.

All novels can be enjoyed as standalone stories.

The stone mason Gerry Riordan appears in *Unshackled and Succession* under his chosen name of Gerry Gleeson.

If any interested reader would like to know more about me and my Australian background, please access my following sites:

My website
www.michaelbeashel.com.au

Australian History Videos on YouTube
https://www.youtube.com/channel/UCLETK6K05kne4xhKChBaVAA

Facebook
https://www.facebook.com/MichaelBeashelAuthor

Goodreads
https://www.goodreads.com/author/show/16827192.Michael_Beashel

Printed in Dunstable, United Kingdom